GREENWAY

Four Mystery Short Stories
Set on Greenway, Agatha Christie's
Holiday Home in Devon

by

gay toltl kinman

Also by gay toltl kinman

MYSTERY NOVELS

Jo Peters Mysteries: Cases as Assistant District Attorney, City Attorney, and P. I.
Tony Reynolds, CIA Agent: Cozy Thriller Stories
Vengeance Is Mine: 9 cases that are based on real cases—but with a twist
A Man Of Honor: A Marlowe and LAPD Officer Agnes Graham Mystery
Stand Down, Mystery Stories
Death in Hollywood 1942: The Marlowe and LAPD Officer Agnes Graham Series
Death in...17 Mysteries
Death in Hamburg
Murder and Mayhem at The Huntington Library
Wolf Castle (originally published as Castle Reiner)
Death in Rancho Las Amigas
Upclose and Personal
Death in Covent Garden
Death in A Small Town
Greeenway, An Elm Short Mystery

CHILDREN'S MYSTERIES

The Adventures of Lauren Macphearson
Lauren Macphearson and The Scottish Adventure
Lauren Macphearson and The Colorado Adventure
Lauren Macphearson and The Jumbled Cupboard Adventure
Lauren Macphearson and The Ghostly Adventure

Super Sleuth: Five Alison Leigh Powers Mysteries
The Mystery of The Missing Arabian
The Mystery of The Missing Miniature Books
The Mystery of The Octagon House
The Secret of The Equestrian Park
The Secret of The Strange Staircase

Gilly's Divorce or Don't Make The Mistakes I Did

NON-FICTION

Desserticide II: AKA Just Desserts and Deathly Advice
Gilly's Manual and Advice on Coping with Your Divorce

PLAYS

The Play's The Thing: A Collection of Plays

A Little Theater Mystery
Death In Russia
Putting Mother's Seat Belt On
Revenge
The Audition
The Mystery Writer
The Thief
Wicked Well
The Purloined Letter
Not One More Word
The Ashes of Zane Grey
Baskets to Jade
Esther Howland: Queen Of Hearts
(A Ten-Minute Biographical Play)
Esther Howland: Queen Of Hearts
(A One-Act Biographical Play)
Nicholas Owen: Builder Of Secret Places
(A Ten-Minute Biographical Play)
Nicholas Owen: Finder Of Secret Places
(A One-Act Biographical Play)
Home Sweet Murder
Mr. Marshall's Doppelganger
The Deposition
Unscheduled Changeover in Hamburg 1974

And, many Mystery Short Stories and Travel Diaries, all available on Kindle at amazon.com.

Editing & Proofreading by William R. Kinman
Cover Designed by Peggie Chan
Photo of gay toltl kinman by Brian and Lilly Loo Studios
Interfacing with Kindle and Amazon by Peggie Chan

Cover photo: Wikipedia: Agatha Christie's House
(File: Greenway_-_Agatha_Christie's_House_(26192476850).jpg)

Published in the United States of America
By Mysterious Women

Dedicated to
Barbara Murray Holt
in appreciation for friendship and Englishisms.

TABLE OF CONTENTS

The first in the series when the narrator, an American scriptwriter with a Los Angeles-based film company, arrives at Greenway to film a documentary about the house and its famous owner—Agatha Christie. Greenway is her property on the River Dart in Devon. A murderer is on the loose—and the narrator is in the way.

Published by Elm Books.

The American film crew revisits Greenway to tell the story of the murders, which occurred the previous May, when they were filming the documentary. The narrator, the crew's American scriptwriter, is living in an apartment that adjoins the main house. She is joined by a person whom she, Kevin their English producer, and Peter the director, think is a famous person. That person says someone is trying to kill her. The trio has to cope with this and still film under a deadline. And a dead line it is.

Published by Mysterious Women on Kindle.

This mystery short story follows *Greenway Revisited* during May while the American film crew is still on the grounds. Kevin, their London producer, is surprised by a woman who says she's his half-sister—same father. The half-sister, whom the narrator names Madame Orange because of her hair, has some Agatha Christie letters, which may be stolen or forged. The letters cause murderous results.

Published by Mysterious Women on Kindle.

The fourth in the series has the narrator and Kevin, the American film company's London-based producer, investigating possible forged Agatha Christie letters. A trio of Christie aficionados wants to copy her letters and sell them as replicas. But not all is as it appears.

Published by Mysterious Women on Kindle.

GREENWAY
A mystery short story

Traveling down the river Dart on a smallish ferry boat, Kevin, our English producer, pointed to the house high above us through the trees. I only caught a glimpse—boxy, rectangular two-story cream-colored that had been Agatha Christie's holiday home—now a shrine. Kevin was impassive, but he'd been here before, as had Peter, the director. Contrary to Kevin, Peter always had a little smile on his face as though he knew a secret no one else did.

In a way he did. He had met Agatha Christie.

I had only met my other five co-workers on the documentary crew at the Los Angeles airport just before we took off for London to film Agatha Christie's house and gardens. Their names were a blur, no time for mnemonics. The only one I knew was Derek as I had worked with him once on a documentary. When we arrived at Greenway, our small crew would be joined by a British one.

Peter had opted for the crew to arrive by ferry, saying that we would get a better feel for the place on the water route. The equipment would be coming by land.

It was the last week of May, lovely day, short-sleeve weather, the beginning of our four-week stay at Torquay in Devon, in the south west part of England. The ferry unloaded us at a tiny wooden dock then chugged off to its other stops. We passed a few picnic tables scattered about to a parade line of half a dozen golf carts. They were driven by volunteers, seniors, who helped with loading, belying their age.

Estrella, the driver of the cart I climbed onto, had a halo of black hair and a sweet smile. Peter apparently knew her and plied her with questions about what changes had been made in the house. I was more interested in the trees, shrubs, and flowers—definitely the 'green' of 'Greenway.' Estrella approached the house, went around the back of it, and then swung onto the driveway in front.

In front of the house on the other side of the driveway, white wooden deck chairs, of the 1930s type, were set out on the lawn as they had been in Christie's day for relaxing, sunning or just enjoying the magnificent view of the estuary above the trees on the hillside. It was the opposite view Kevin had pointed out from the ferry.

We stepped down off the carts and were ushered toward the entrance, some of us taking a minute to view the house up close.

I was very grateful that all of the volunteers wore name tags. I didn't know how *hey you* translated over here. I tried to memorize some of their names in case they didn't wear their badge the next time I encountered them. Ethel was a sprite. Nora looked like the stereotypical English aunt, Prunella—well, she looked like her name, wizened and prune-like, sharp nosed, and giving orders—also sharply. Clarissa had a thick head of black hair like my driver, Estrella. Possibly they were sisters—only Clarissa had more bird-like movements.

The man who opened the door was gnome-like, round-shouldered and hunched over. Smiling, he said, "Mrs. Christie welcomes you to her home. My name is Jeremy. Come in, come in."

We trooped in.

For me, a writer, it would be hard to top the thrill of walking through Agatha Christie's house. It was like being in a church that was famous, revered, and one that I had longed to see. Awe was the best word.

A National Trust guidebook gave the lay of the house and the land noting that Agatha had spent holidays here—summers and Christmas with her family "so it was a happy place for her." It was a large house—six rooms on the first floor—the ground floor to the Brits—and the same on the second floor—which was called the first.

In our packet of background information, I had read that Christie had said whenever she wanted to add another room or remodel she had to sell a story. *I don't quite believe that, Agatha.* I thought. *I believe you wrote because you had to—and not for the money.*

How cool would it be to write a mystery set in Greenway, I wondered. Poirot or Miss Marple or Mrs. Oliver, aka Apple Ariadne, on the spot to investigate? Forget frivolous Tommy and Tuppence, they would be of no use.

Our volunteers escorted us on a walk-through of the house. Each took a different route—and they knew their Christie, I quickly learned. They knew about the plots and characters in her books, about her life and about everything that was in the house. I had read Christie, but I was not in their league. These people even knew the American and the often different British titles for all of her works.

Bits of information floated into my brain as I heard the other guides whenever our paths crossed, or when Estrella took a breath in her explanation. The volunteers *lived* Christie. Every item, from table cloth to rug, from picture to bowl, had a story—where it was purchased, why, and for how much. My jet-lagged brain tried to remember it all. The others had glazed eyes, as I'm sure I did, except for Derek. Glimpses of him told me he was mentally framing shots.

We all assembled in the summer dining room to view a map of the area. Not just any old map, but one that pinpointed where all the fictional murders had been committed. Agatha mined the area for settings, including her own Boathouse.

My thoughts turned to her disappearance. After finding her car abandoned in December of 1926, over one thousand police officers and volunteers combed the country looking for the author, until she was found, safe and sound, eleven days later. The entire affair could have made for a lovely mystery, but she never wrote the plot—only lived it—and never ever spoke of it. How long would she have stayed away if she hadn't been discovered? Had she thought past the charade—possibly that wandering husband Archie, who had been suspected of doing away with her, would hang? As intriguing as it was, none of that would be in the documentary. The house was the focus, and she hadn't owned it with Archie.

The documentary was to be a visual tour highlighting some of the items in each of the rooms, and how she lived when she was there. In addition to the summer dining room, which was in the front of the house with a view of the river and hills, there was a winter dining room next to the kitchen.

I enjoyed the volunteers' asides as the film crew worked. The scriptwriters had taken poetic license with a specific mundane item that was to be shown, trying to make it seem like more than it was. I was the writer on location so that if there were any glitches, I could change the words, and there always were a few. Luckily, I didn't have to dash off to do research, as I had a bevy of experts to call on. They were politely silent unless an error was spoken, which would result in frantic hand waving out of camera range, and an immediate correction.

The filming was going along well when the first murder occurred.

We would never have heard about it down here in Torquay, save for the headlines of the local newspaper which read, "The Mysterious Affair at Styles." The headline was the same as the title of a Christie book. Only this murder was for real. Mrs. Inglethorpe, the matriarch of the estate, had been poisoned, just as in Christie's mystery.

The next morning in the dining room I noticed someone had put a red star on the map on where *The Mysterious Affair at Styles* was labeled.

No details of the poisoning of the most recently-deceased Mrs. Inglethorpe at Styles were forthcoming, so no comparison was made with the book even though the huddle of volunteers did their best to make one.

A bit of rain set back our filming outside. Derek wanted to hike himself over to Styles Court to pick up any information he could. Kevin and Peter consented to two days only. We didn't know how long the rain would last. Since Derek did most of the outside filming, he was expendable. Besides we were all curious what was going on over there. Peter and Kevin must have been curious too, although they didn't let on.

The next day, there was another red star on the map. This was next to the title *Curtain,* which had also been set at Styles Court when Poirot visited there in his declining years. The newest victim, Mr. Norton, had been shot and had the same name as Christie's victim in *Curtain*, who had been shot also.

In the coffee room, an area set aside for the staff and volunteers, there was already a discussion.

"...they're both set at Styles Court..."

"...but *Curtain* was published in 1975, Styles in 1920..."

"...she could have written them about the same time. It was one of those manuscripts she put in the bank vault to be published when she ran out of ideas..."

"...we don't know when she wrote it. Probably about the time she said she was sick of Poirot..."

I was learning a lot. Nice to write so fast that an author can stow manuscripts in a bank vault.

Back to the dining room, I went, followed by some of the volunteers. Next on the map was *The Patriotic Murders*. "Not a novel, but a collection of short stories," Nora, the aunt-type, informed me.

While listening to her, I remembered what she had told me about herself. She had never married. Her fiancé had died in one of England's wars. But she still wore her engagement ring—and had worked her entire adult life until retiring ten years ago. The ladies of her era never sat fully on the chair, only on the front half of the seat. "When I went to work after he was killed, my supervisor told me, 'You may sit on the entire seat, Nora, as we've paid for the whole chair, not just a portion of it.'" It took me a moment to catch on, and then I laughed at the thought of buying only part of a chair.

"Next will be," Ethel, the sprite, said, interrupting my laughter, and putting her finger on the map's glass over *Spider's Web*.

"No," said Estrella, sharply, behind her.

After a moment, "Ah," was uttered by Ethel.

"Why?" I asked after waiting few moments.

"A play," said Estrella. "The murderer is only doing books."

"There'll be more?" I focused on the map again. "I thought it was just at Styles."

Ethel and Nora murmured together, reinforcing my idea of a Greek chorus. They moved off, shaking their heads, not answering my question.

Funerals are Fatal looked like the next one on the map.

But I was wrong. It was Mr. Clark of Churston from *The ABC Murders*. I was informed by the chorus that apparently the murderer had cut to the chase in that he skipped the locations A for Andover and B for Bexhill that were in the book.

Churston was a stone's throw from Torquay—at least that's what it looked like on the map. I was getting nervous. The murderer was getting closer. None of the volunteers seemed concerned by this. They were quite clinical in their observations.

I asked about *Funerals*.

"Too far inland," said Estrella.

Oh.

"I still don't think he should have done the second murder at Styles. We don't know when it was written and put away. Does Jeremy know?" Estrella asked the bevy of ladies. Jeremy was the door-gnome.

"Well, it's done, so there's nothing we can do about that,' was the retort.

"But it's out of order," Estrella reiterated.

"Yes, but it's along the coast," Nora commented. The Greek chorus was quiet as they all looked at the map. Alas, they were right. One of the points of the red star on Churston touched Torquay.

I was sitting on the story of the century, right here filming the Christie house, while real murders were imitating the fictional ones. What was I going to do about it? What I wanted to do was skedaddle back home to Los Angeles as quickly as I could.

"It's out of order publication-wise, but it's near the coast toward here, Torquay, which means you know what's next." They all looked at the map, and then at each other nodding.

"What?" I said loudly enough to make some of them jump.

The Greek chorus said *Dead Man's Folly*.

"The plot happened here and it was filmed here, dear," Estrella patted my arm.

After *Folly,* the map told me the next one was *Murder at Hazelmoor*, yes, really close, then *Elephants Can Remember,* and *The Peril at End House.*

"*Elephants* is another one that was put in the bank vault," Estrella said. "But she hadn't invented Ariadne yet, so perhaps just the plot was put away. Then *Peril at End House*, another Ariadne one." She paused. "That's if he's going down the coast."

I knew she was referring to the murderer.

Dame Agatha usually had about seven suspects, every one of them with a motive for killing off the head of the clan, so inheritances could be distributed *tout de suite.* Too many suspects. The Thin Man movie series had William Powell as Nick Charles assembling everyone in the living room or office. "You could have done it because it was your gun," he would say menacingly to the first person. The movie viewer always knew it wasn't that person because there were at least six more suspects to go. "But it wasn't you because you told the truth—your gun was stolen—by…. Then on to the next suspect.

Clamminess crept along the back of my neck as I realized there were at least seven hard-core volunteers surrounding the map, the six ladies and Jeremy. Was this a *Murder on the Orient Express* situation where all of the travelers had a hand in the death?

Even though the volunteers were all older, they were quite agile from what I had seen of what they did around the house and slinging our equipment on the golf cars. Poisoning and shooting a gun would be child's play for them.

Breaking into my thoughts was Derek, who had just returned from Styles. We adjourned to the coffee room where he brought us up to date in the two Styles Court deaths. Yes, Mrs. Inglethorpe was poisoned, as in *Affair*, and Mr. Norton was shot, as in *Curtain*. Fiction and real life were the same.

After Derek finished, Ethel, stated that she had a nephew who was a police officer in Churston, and she had been talking to him. We all leaned toward her, and collectively seemed to be holding our breath, waiting to get the latest news. Ethel seemed reticent to tell all. I'd labeled her as a sprite, as she was the most vivacious of the group with a marvelous sense of humor in her asides that one had to be close by to catch. She had a mop of grey-brown, frizzy hair that she wore in different styles. This time she wore a ponytail on the top of her head, so that each time she moved the 'tail' flopped to a different place, sometimes even over her face. It was almost hard to concentrate on what she was saying.

"Even though all the murders were not in the same jurisdiction, the information went into a nation-wide database," Ethel instructed us as her top knot pony tail swung to and fro. "The third murder," she said, "the one at Churston, had raised a few eyebrows with comments made about the Christie connection, as the murders were hardly a coincidence. But others felt that it was too farfetched to consider." That was all she knew, or all that her nephew would tell her.

"Jeremy, wasn't *Curtain* written long before it was published?" Estrella said. She had mentioned this earlier.

Jeremy perked up, warming to the subject. "It was written about thirty years before, in the 1940s. Agatha mentioned the idea in *Peril at End House*, chapter nine, and probably thought about it in 1935 or so. She wanted to be able to kill off her detective and not have him picked up by someone else."

"She killed him off and left the manuscript in the bank vault?" I asked, still amazed at the thought of her productivity.

"That is quite correct," Jeremy nodded in assent.

"But in *Curtain,* there were two murders, Franklin and Norton," Nora said.

"That's true, dear lady, but Barbara Franklin committed suicide, according to Poirot's testimony. He wanted no investigation because he planned to do away with the real murderer, Norton, who had been responsible for several deaths prior in other areas. A serial murderer. Poirot shot him."

"Hard to believe that Poirot murdered someone," Nora said.

"He considered his action stopped more killing. Poirot knew that with his deteriorating heart, he hadn't the stamina, at that point, to investigate and prove the man a killer." Jeremy smiled.

I noted how Jeremy spoke of the fictional characters as thought they had really lived—he believed it. Well—so did the others.

Prunella interrupted. "Jeremy, I called you Wednesday night, but your telephone machine wasn't on, and your mobile was shut off."

Jeremy's eyes darted to the right, then to the left then back to the right. "Not on, you say? Wednesday?" he said. "What was it you wanted?"

"Just to remind you to be here an hour earlier." Prunella said.

"Ah, must've got to bed early that night so I'd be sure to be here." Jeremy winked at the rest of the ladies.

"Weren't sure you'd remember the new schedule," she said.

I could see a little tightening of lips because I knew Prunella had reminded everyone at least twice about the earlier starting time to accommodate our filming, as Peter wanted the natural light of early morning. Barely five feet tall, as big as a minute, my grandmother would say, and she walked with a limp. Precision was her game, probably why she was in charge of scheduling. A martinet, but the soul of efficiency. I sure appreciated that, having just worked in Greece where time was malleable.

If I was to pick a suspect from the volunteers who could plan and execute the murders, Prunella would be it. But why would she do it?

"Mrs. Christie was named Clarissa, as was her grandmother, her mother, and then her daughter," Clarissa said. Definitely another non sequitur but it broke the tension.

"You were named after her?" I said slightly surprised.

"Not really, although I like to say so," she said with a shy smile. "It's a family name, quite a few Clarissas here. She looked around as though she might spot one.

While we, the film crew, were here, the house was closed to visitors. Repair work was going on at the Boathouse, so that was not open to the public either. People in boats plying up and down the river Dart would normally be allowed to dock and picnic on the tables there. However, now there was a big sign stating the area was closed for repairs, no landing allowed, and that the dock was not safe. I think the latter was more of a warning to the would-be looky-loos. I didn't think it was true, but it seemed to work. All the same, I wasn't going to take a short walk on it to find out.

While the crew was having lunch, most of the chorus followed me back to the dining room where I looked at the map again. "What's interesting…," said Clarissa, then a long pause. Suspense for me! "…is that the titles on the map are the American ones. *Funerals Are Fatal* was *After The Funeral*, and *Murder at Hazelmoor* was *Sittaford Mystery* here in the U.K."

"What does that have to do with the price of tea in China? Ethel asked.

"Just an observation," said Clarissa, with a big sigh.

12

"*Dead Man's Folly* is next then," Ethel said, reiterating what I'd learned earlier. "And it was right here, using our Boathouse."

Before I could ponder that, the chorus swirled around, reminding me of the time I was on a farm where there were a lot of peacocks. I had gone to look at an old building, and when I turned around there was an array of peacocks, probably more curious than I was. It was a heart-stopping moment. Were they going to attack me like in Alfred Hitchcock's *The Birds*? Would they peck me to death? I waved my arms and said "Shoo, shoo." They had parted like the Red Sea—peacock blue in this case.

That was what the group of the ladies reminded me of. Were they evil or benign? They seemed to swirl and eddy around me when I was in the house. Was I such a curiosity? Or did they have other reasons for following me? Trying to make me a Christie aficionado? Educating me on Christie? Or making sure I didn't pilfer anything? Especially the silver pieces which Agatha and Max had collected, one for each year from 1648 to 1837. None of the other crew members seemed to attract such attention, but then I was the only one who didn't have anything to do. The crew was always in a group filming.

"In *Folly*, Mr. Poirot did research on the family and found out there were some connections, so that the murder of poor Marlene Tucker—she was only 14—had relevance," said Clarissa.

"Fourteen going on thirty," Estrella murmured.

"Don't speak ill of the dead," Clarissa said to her sister.

They all laughed for the 'dead' in this case was fictional.

I didn't laugh because I was too busy gasping. "Tucker?" I asked.

"Yes, my dear.' Clarissa patted my arm.

My first married name had been Tucker.

And here I was near the Boathouse. If the killer followed the pattern he or she had set, then another Tucker was about to be murdered there—me.

I realized that the motive for the individual deaths was nothing personal, only how it fitted in with the Christie novels. Someone was imitating the fictional Christie murders. The murders were about the name of victim and the location. Which meant—a Tucker had to be killed in the Boathouse.

The ratiocination of Poirot and Marple were badly needed now.

I tried to analyze this objectively. No one wanted to kill *me*, only someone with the same name as the Christie victim. That was true in all the other cases. Which meant—looking at the overall motive. Someone who wanted to use the pattern of murders for a reason. I considered what possible motive that could be. Who would gain—and what?

I moved away from the group and went outside to sit on a white deck chair. No one followed.

My thoughts logically of the motives were:

1) To publicize the documentary. Suspects would be Kevin and Peter. I had to admit it was a whopper of a PR plan. Or even Derek. After all, he was in Styles when the second murder there was committed—the shooting of Mr. Norton. But they were all well-known in the industry, and had not lack of jobs. It wasn't as though they needed to jump-start their careers. But still—a big hit in the documentary field wouldn't hurt. Maybe even an Oscar.

2) Recognition for someone with a puffed up ego. Someone who wanted his or her superior knowledge of Christie to be recognized. That could be any of the volunteers. I considered the two sisters, Estrella and Clarissa, which reminded me of *Arsenic and Old Lace*. The two sisters in the movie were doing in old men with a dose of arsenic. They thought

they were doing the men a favor, as they—the men—had nothing to live for.

Or Jeremy, the gnome; Ethel, the sprite; Nora, the aunt; Prunella, the martinet. Prunella—yes! She could be the mastermind, scheduling and ordering everyone about. But she didn't try to impress anyone with the knowledge. She was more interested in a well-working machine that of her volunteers.

Or all of them working together a la *Murder on the Orient Express.* That made more sense—so Christie-like. Ah—I just couldn't see it.

3) Some maniacal person who was taunting the police for some reason that made sense only to him or her.

I didn't have to solve the murders—I wasn't Poirot or Marple. I just wanted to know who to watch out for.

I hoped the police were looking beyond each murder victim to the bigger picture. One motive for all, obviously someone with deranged thinking, but clever.

Kevin called to me, which made me jump. The crew was starting to film in the summer dining room. The map was to be featured and discussed. Much to be made of the Boathouse, where the victim, Marlene Tucker, 14, was found strangled with a rope in *Dead Man's Folly.*

I wanted to defy the gods and go down to the Boathouse. But I was not going to. The murderer would have to work to get my body down there. He or she could try to force me at gunpoint but *I ain't doin' it.* I knew the person was set on killing me, so I wasn't going to make it easy.

The star of the show was interviewing Jeremy about the map, all in the script. No mention was made of the real murders, because they hadn't been committed when the script was written. And I certainly wasn't going to suggest those changes. It wasn't pertinent to the tour of the house documentary.

Later, when the crew was filming in the garden, or so I thought, I was reading in the comfortable chair in the large hallway ready for any call. Then I heard Estrella's voice. "I've come to fetch you, dear."

"Does Peter want a script change?"

"Peter wants you down at the Boathouse."

"I thought Peter was filming in the Peach House and garden."

"I've me orders." She patted the walkie-talkie on her belt.

"Peter called you on that?" Only staff and volunteers had them.

"No, Jeremy did. Said Peter gave the order."

Was I going to tear down to the Boathouse, script and pen in hand, in the golf cart Estrella was driving? No way. God could have delivered the message in person and my answer would still be the same. Not on my life!

"Thank you. I'll check with Peter to see exactly what he wants."

She seemed disappointed, but not as if I'd thwarted her plans. If she had any.

I could easily walk over to the garden to see Peter. I sank back in the chair to think for a moment. What did I want to do? I could ignore the request, go back to the Inn and my soft, inviting pillow—which would prolong the agony of waiting for someone to try to kill me.

I wanted to get on a plane and go home as far from the Boathouse as possible.

Ignoring Peter's request was fantasy. I couldn't do that. But I could take the bull by the horns—arming myself with a weapon. Maybe a knife from the kitchen. The better part of valor was to retreat to the Inn so that I could live—literally—to fight another day. Instead, I made my way to the kitchen. The selection of knives would not make any chef proud. I heard someone in the hallway, so just grabbed a knife, then a tea towel to wrap it in it and quickly stuck in my backpack. There was no one in the hallway.

Duty and curiosity sped me on my way to the Peach House, where Peter was indeed filming.

"Did you want me to go down at the Boathouse?"

"Great idea. See if anything's changed. The workers aren't doing renovations, just repairs but something could be altered."

Great idea? That didn't sound like he had given an order. All of a sudden, I felt dizzy. Someone was lying. I must have swayed because Peter grabbed my arm. "You're looking quite pale. Go back to the Inn for a rest. You can check it tomorrow." Then the faithful Estrella in her golf cart was there.

I did go back to the Inn and my soft pillow, but my head was whirling with thoughts. Who was lying? Estrella? Jeremy? Someone who gave the message to Jeremy? Or someone told Estrella Jeremy had a message? Too many variables. What would have happened at the Boathouse if I'd gone down? I was curious, but not that curious. Curiosity killed the cat, but satisfaction brought it back. It be the other way around for me. Satisfied, I would be floating around in the ethereal with the other spirits.

Later, at the Inn, there was a knock on my door. I grabbed my robe and tied it on quickly before opening the door and peering over the chain lock.

Jeremy and Estrella. "Estrella told me you were unwell. I brought you some of my mother's tonic." He handed me a paper bag with a bottle in it. Estrella, giggling, clung to his arm.

I pulled the bottle out. Brandy. From a famous distillery. The cap and seal intact. I laughed. "What a wonderful mother you have."

"Guaranteed to fix you up straightway. Even if you have a broken leg." His grin was almost from ear to ear, making him more gnome-like. Estrella looked like she'd already had some of the same tonic.

"At home, chicken soup does exactly that," I said.

"That's good, too. Take the tonic in hot water with a pinch of sugar. A few drops of lemon will make it even better."

"Thanks so much, Jeremy, Estrella. So thoughtful. I feel better already." I clutched at the neck of my robe with one hand and the paper bag with the other.

He gave a little wave, pivoted Estrella about and headed for the stairs. Curious, as I don't drink. Perhaps he didn't know that. The brandy, whether tainted or not, would not be going down my gullet. I'd give it to someone. But what if it was tainted? Another problem for another day. I'd just throw it out.

I thought about asking Jeremy about the call that Estrella had relayed to me. If he didn't do it, he wouldn't know what I was talking about. If he did it, he'd know by now I knew Peter hadn't asked him—or Estrella—to call. Then another thought—what if Peter had been the one lying to me?

The next morning, back at Greenway. Everyone was enjoying the beautiful day. They were all in a good mood. It had been a happy place for Agatha, now for them, too. If one didn't think about the murders.

Filming at the Boathouse was scheduled for today. However, Jeremy had an announcement about the police catching some bank robbers who were hiding out in there. "No one can go down there, even I. A police officer guarding the path." Jeremy seemed quite miffed, the lord of the manor forbidden access to his own property.

Peter was flexible, shots in the gardens—the South Walled Garden, the Vinery, the North Walled Garden, the Fernery, the Hydrangea Walk and a few others that had photogenic statuary. As we all went out there, Estrella said, "Everyone is so excited about this documentary. Jeremy feels he's finally getting his due as a Christie expert. He really does know a lot. You should see his cottage. It's all filled with Christie memorabilia. Of course, he has all of her books and the various editions."

"There are a lot of experts here."

"Oh, yes, many. All of us volunteers fancy ourselves to be experts."

"Did any of you ever meet her?" I knew Peter had but he didn't put himself out there as an expert, only as an aficionado.

She said no, and shook her head sadly. I gave her a moment to grieve over that lost opportunity. Then I pulled out the script and quizzed her about any changes to the Boathouse. I didn't have to go there to inspect, I had an expert at hand.

The next day we got the all-clear sign. We were all to go down there, riding in golf carts driven by the volunteers. Safety in numbers, I told myself. If the whole crew wasn't in on the murders, then I was safe.

Thinking about a giant conspiracy made a lot of sense. That meant everyone had alibis for all but one of the murders—the one they committed, so they'd never be a suspect. The motive—to make the documentary a hit, and everyone associated with it famous. I looked around at the crew. No way. They worked in unison, not that they always agreed, but I couldn't see a giant conspiracy.

The faithful volunteers were there, loading up the carts and taking their passengers carefully down the steep path to the Boathouse. Derek and I were on Jeremy's. I didn't say anything about the brandy, still in its paper bag, but reposing in the bathroom trash.

Well—here I was at the Boathouse. Now what? I'd just been sitting around, as there was hardly anything for me to do. I had verified that everything in the script about the Boathouse was still correct. Peter wasn't one to keep changing the script. He was a company man, and always liked to bring projects in on time and under budget. Peter had no sense of humor, in spite of the slight smile he always had. He was almost mechanical, but he was good. No temper tantrums or fits, just nice and steady—you could count on him. Not mercurial like some directors changing from Dr. Jekyll to Mr. Hyde in the blink of an eye. I won't say he was fun to work for, but it wasn't stressful either. But that didn't mean I was taking him off my suspect list.

We worked until 7 p.m. The light was fading, and so was I, even though I just sat around all day. Derek couldn't find one of his expensive lenses and was looking for it. He told Jeremy and me what it looked like and where he had been—all over. So the three of us scrabbled around looking for it. Finally Jeremy shouted that he had found it. We were the last, everyone at least half an hour gone. Not good.

I plunked down in the front seat of the cart. Derek, at the back of the cart, made a sound like a sigh. I turned around to see him slump to the ground.

"Aren't you going to help your friend?" Jeremy asked as he looked up.

"What?"

Then I saw the hypodermic needle in Jeremy's hand. He must have switched ampules after he injected Derek. If I leaned over Derek, I'd get an armful too. Something to knock me out, not kill me—yet—for if my suspicious were right, I was supposed to die with a rope around my neck. Like the young Miss Tucker.

"You hid Derek's lens so everyone would leave before us," I said.

"A necessity," Jeremy answered.

"You murdered all those people," I said it as a statement.

"A necessity," he said again.

"Why a necessity?"

"So that I'll be famous. Finally recognized as the world's leading expert on Greenway and Agatha Christie."

"You killed all those people just for that? Recognition?"

"Quite clever, wasn't it?

"When they find out you are the murderer, they'll cut your part and substitute someone else."

"The murderer in this case will be Derek."

"You're going to pin all those murders on Derek?"

"I've made sure he had no alibi for those nights. And the police will find adequate evidence in his room—souvenirs taken from each victim." Jeremy came around from the back of the cart and Derek's prone body. "And now I need something from you. But first, you need some of this." He held up the syringe. And hard not to notice the coil of rope around his left arm.

"Then a bit of rope around my neck like the Tucker girl?"

"You did figure it out," he said.

"How did you know my name had been Tucker?"

"An old film credit you had. It's noted on IMDb."

Oh. It was a website that listed all credits of everyone. I used it the beginning flush of marriage to my first husband—so charming but useless. Little did he know he would be responsible for my untimely demise.

"Don't think I'm ready to go yet."

"It's unavoidable, my dear, don't fight it," he said.

I pulled out the kitchen knife. "I am going to fight. You are not taking me easily." If only I had learned martial arts, kicking the hypo out of his hand. Or Cane Fu—using the cane's handle to attack his throat, then thrusting the other end through the ribs.

Derek groaned. No wonder—he'd fallen on his bulky camera case. Even unconscious he must be uncomfortable.

I thought of taking off, running up the path, but it was steep. Running and yelling for help was not possible. Besides Jeremy had the cart—and the key. I stood my ground.

"We'll just have to go to Plan B," Jeremy said,

I didn't have a Plan B. I hadn't expected to even use Plan A—the kitchen knife. It had a broad blade. I could inflict some damage if I got close enough. But the idea was to keep him away. Particularly from my neck—meaning that my neck and his rope should not meet.

He hesitated, as well he should have. He had to rid me of the knife. I was holding it with both hands ready to cleave his balding skull in two. Was it sharp enough to even cut his skin? Probably only make a dent, a minor impression that would disappear after a few minutes. He slipped the hypo into his pocket and pulled a length or rope from the coil. I moved to the front of the cart, keeping it between us. He moved away from the prone Derek. He snapped the rope at me like a bullwhip. It hit one of the rods holding up the roof of the cart. I backed away more around the other side, getting closer to Derek.

He followed, snapping the rope again. It made a scary noise but not much else. My heart was beating so fast I was getting dizzy. I had to hold out. We could keep circling the wagon forever. I could tell he was thinking fast. This wasn't working for him.

"Why don't you help me get your friend into the cart? We'll take him back to the house where he can sleep off his stupor."

"Jeremy, you need a new script writer." I could hardly get the words out, my mouth was so dry.

"How about this?" He went back to Derek while I moved back to the front of the cart. He slipped the rope under Derek's neck, put his foot on his back—hard to do since Derek's back was a mound over the camera case. "Drop the knife and come here or your friend dies."

"How do I know you won't kill him anyhow?"

"I need him to be the murderer. I told you that." Jeremy was getting testy, into the Mr. Hyde state. "One quick pull and he's a goner."

"Then what are you going to do for a murderer?"

"I guess you'll have to be it. Hanged yourself in the Boathouse because of what you'd done. Remorse. All those murders. The evidence will be in your room, not Derek's." Big grin.

Yes, he could pull that off. "Good script, Jeremy. Yes, that will work, with a little tweaking."

"Tweaking? It doesn't need any tweaking. What's wrong with it?"

Plots weren't coming to me as fast as they had to Agatha. What if I rushed him, yelling Bonsai or something.

"When will we be found? In the morning? How are you going to explain where you were? You were last seen with us."

"I'll think of something. Hurry up, we're running out of time. I'm pulling tighter."

Derek groaned again. It startled Jeremy so that he dropped one end of the rope. But he soon had it in hand again.

"Do you want me to write a note? Confessing all?" I said.

"Nice delay tactic. No note is necessary. Drop the knife and come here."

All of a sudden there were lights and a lot of people coming out of the bushes. *Birnam Wood doth come to Dunsinane.*

"That's enough, Jeremy. You may drop the rope now. You are surrounded by the police. Any further action on your part and you will be seriously wounded."

Since all the police officers were pointing serious looking guns at him, it was no idle threat. A woman in uniform came up to me and tried to pry the knife out of my hands. It wasn't that I wasn't willing to give it up, it's just that I was clutching it so hard that it was now molded to my hands. "You're safe now, Miss," the police officer said.

Derek groaned for the third time. Little wonder as Jeremy was still holding the rope taut. Then Jeremy dropped it. If he had he tried to garrote Derek, I'm sure he would have been riddled with bullets like in an old-time gangster movie.

Jeremy was searched thoroughly, syringe carefully removed, handcuffed, and literally carted off in the golf cart.

"We'll see that you and your friend get back all right," the officer in charge said. I sank down to the ground, my legs no longer performing well. "He's been drugged," I said, nodding toward the unconscious Derek.

"Yes, we heard everything and recorded it."

I looked around. "But how?"

"Truth be told, we concocted the story about the bank robbers hiding out here and closed off the area. It was the only way we could reasonably have time for our technicians to install the cameras and sound equipment."

If I hadn't been sitting, I would be now—in amazement. "You did know all those murders were related to the Agatha Christie stories?"

"It seemed outlandish, but we don't reject any theories. The second murder at Styles confirmed it. Logically there would be one in the Boathouse but we didn't know when or who."

"Someone named Tucker," I said.

"I presume that's you, Miss."

"Yep. Thanks a lot for saving our lives."

Two golf carts arrived. They carefully loaded Derek and his equipment on one and left.

"I'm still a little wobbly." I was helped up and settled into the other cart.

"We'll see you back to the Inn. You will have to testify, although we certainly have enough evidence to convict," the officer in charge continued.

"Sure," I answered, "As long as the courtroom isn't in the Boathouse."

~The End~

GREENWAY REVISITED
A mystery short story

Kevin, our London producer, asked me to write a segment on the apartment ('holiday cottage,' the National Trust called it) that was for rent in Agatha Christie's home. I was happy to have the writing credit, the money—and sleeping in Agatha Christie's house for two weeks was icing on the luscious cake.

I think Kevin offered a deal to the National Trust, by paying for the rent on the apartment and filming an infomercial to publicize the National Trust's four holiday rentals on Greenway. That was in return for the film crew taking over the property again. We were filming the reenactment of the attempted murders that occurred here last May, while we were making a documentary about the house. That script had been written in California, where I lived. I was here, as I had been last time, to make any changes in the script that Peter, the director, felt were necessary. He rarely changed anything.

Alas, the infomercial script Kevin had promised had to be written and ready to film before the end of two weeks. That meant I wouldn't be doing much lollygagging around my temporary digs trying to commune with Agatha. I had to set my derriere on a chair with my fingers poised over the keyboard of my laptop. The truth was—I was in seventh heaven to be able to stay there at all.

Eerie in a way, to be here this May to relive the attempted murders from last May. The writers had treated it as another Christie plot—and it could have been. Agatha would have loved it. I had no doubt she was sitting in a comfortable cloud watching it all and chortling.

She had a sense of humor—had to in her life—a beloved mother dying and two wandering husbands. She was known here in the area as Mrs. Mallowan, for she had bought the property with her second husband, Max, the archaeologist. Here she was not Agatha Christie, the author. This was her time away—a holiday—from her profession. Although we writers know the mind is never on vacation.

In the National Trust on-site office I saw a large white board with the names of the cottages, dates and who was or would be occupying them. Curiously, the intended tenant, Miss Chiltern, was listed. Rumor had it that that was the birth name of the Prime Minister, and she was coming to stay for a few days—however she had appendicitis and had to cancel. My writerly mind thought of Kissinger in China during the Nixon years, when he claimed he had the flu but slipped out the back door to meet with the Chinese envoy without the accompaniment of the news staff.

Perhaps it was more prestigious to keep her name up there—definitely more prestigious than mine.

In the apartment I had dropped everything in the first bedroom I saw after I climbed the stairs to the first floor. When I returned I went up another flight to the second floor where the kitchen, living room, two bedrooms and baths were.

On the kitchen counter a bottle of wine stood on a small silver tray with a glass and wine opener. Also fruit salad in a large frosted plastic bowl covered with plastic wrap. It looked lovely but had a myriad of strawberries in it. I was allergic to them. Since the juices had all mixed together, it wouldn't work even if I took the strawberries out. Kevin and

Peter were coming for a meeting, so I could give them a glass of wine and fruit salad.

How nice the National Trust was to their guests! Then it dawned on me—the guest was Miss Chiltern. The flowers in the master bedroom when I'd arrived—a touch of class. But not for me, which meant I couldn't give the wine and fruit salad away. I put the bowl in the refrigerator and the wine on a shelf under the counter, amidst some pots and pans.

I wondered if Miss Chiltern paid, or was this a perk of her job, her being the head of the National Trust, so to speak—since she was the head of everything. And why had she booked to stay here? Was she a devotee of Agatha Christie? This information would make a nice addition to our infomercial—if I could use her name. The Prime Minister slept here! Maybe a plaque would be appropriate.

In the middle of the night I felt hot, even with the window open. I was restless and thought a change of venue might help. The double bed seemed to be too big, too hard. I felt for the flashlight on my nightstand and made my way upstairs, checking out the two bedrooms. I picked one, opened the window, and immediately the door slammed shut. The unexpected noise shot my heart rate up. Then I thought, better now than when I was asleep, so I left it closed.

The bed closest to the window seemed to be the most comfortable, closer to the slight breeze. I picked up the flashlight I had dropped, turned it off, set it on the nightstand, swung my legs onto the bed—and that's the last I remembered.

In the morning I went downstairs to the master bedroom where I had started out last night. I noticed the pillow I had used was on the floor and the bed coverings pulled back almost completely. I was sure I hadn't done that. Had the maid been in early, then realized I was still here and left?

No time to puzzle over that as there was a loud knock at the door, and a moment later it swung open. A man bore a tray laden with a silver coffee service and a folding tray under his arm. "Good morning ma'am. The coffee you ordered." He strode in, unfolded the tray-stand by the window in the master bedroom, set the silver tray on top of it, pulled a chair closer, bowed slightly and left. I heard him trotting down the stairs.

Coffee. That's all there was. Not for me. I was a tea drinker and was dying for a good cup of English tea. Ah well, I could make my own. Back upstairs to the kitchen to fill the electric kettle.

I should move all my stuff up there. I had rushed in yesterday, dumped everything in the first bedroom I saw. I should have checked the layout before I unpacked, not realizing the kitchen and sitting room were up a flight. I hadn't read all the information—but now I would.

Kevin and Peter came over later for our meeting. I thought about heating up the coffee and setting out the silver service with a flourish, but when I went to get it, the tray and all its accoutrements were gone. Even the folding tray—and the chair—was back to where it had been originally.

Luckily, the guys brought their own tall Styrofoam cups of coffee. We settled in at the rectangular kitchen table. Chitchat about how I liked the accommodations. Well—really not chitchat, as Kevin wanted to be sure everything was what he asked for, and as promised by the National Trust. I assured him all was well, and yes, I had slept well. No need to go into details.

We were well into our meeting when someone came up the stairs to the top floor and walked in. We all looked. Blonde hair curled under, slightly below her ears. She looked as surprised to see us as we were to see her. Maid? I didn't think so. NT official checking to be sure there was no orgy going on with one woman and two men in Agatha Christie's guest digs?

After we eyed each other for several moments, she pulled off her hair, or rather, her wig. Not a National Truster, obviously. Her hair was short, brown and curly, much like mine.

"Damned thing itches," she said. She stuffed the wig into a big shoulder bag while still looking at us. Then she fluffed her hair.

"Oh, my god," said Kevin, *sotto voce*.

"What?" I said.

"The P.M," his voice quizzical.

"What!" I shouted. The meaning of P.M. exploded half way between brain and mouth.

"You look incredibly like the P.M.?" He said it as a question, rather than a statement.

"People never recognize me in person," she shot back. "Any coffee?" she asked, and she sat herself on the fourth chair at the table.

Peter popped up like he'd been ejected. "I'll make some."

Meanwhile I stared at the Prime Minister, who really didn't look like her TV image, but closer to it without the blonde wig.

Kevin was wide-eyed. Peter looked like he was happy to have something else to do, like ripping open a packet of instant coffee.

"Don't know who you are, but you don't look like murderers, but that's what I'm on the lookout for. You see—someone's trying to kill me."

After our explanation about who we were, she said, "We gave out the story about appendicitis—everyone's getting it these days—and

31

cancelled the reservations here. However, that didn't get through to the right people, because they called this morning on my mobile about my order for breakfast. So thought I would come down to check it out."

"Someone brought up a coffee service, but it's gone now."

"Good. Hope you didn't drink any. Obviously you didn't. You're here."

It took a moment for what she said to sink in. "You mean—"

Peter brought her mug to the table. "Should be okay, it was in a sealed packet."

"It was all poisoned," she said as she took a sip.

"Wine," I choked out. "A bottle of wine." I pointed." The lower cupboard." Peter opened the cabinet door. It was gone, too. Just the tray and glass still on the counter. "And the fruit salad."

The three of them contemplated me, as though that was a punch line. "The refrigerator." Gone also. Being a teetotaler and allergic to strawberries saved me so I could, perhaps, be poisoned another day.

Her cell phone rang. She stood up and walked away from us. "Yes, yes, fine. I'm here now a. All's well. And I have a roommate. Her name is—" She looked at me quizzically, but Kevin was faster and gave her the list of the crew members, pointing, I presume, to my name.

"She's with a film company. From California." She read the information at the top of the list. "I can't talk now, George. I'll call you back." She disconnected. "My Administrative Assistant," she said as way of explanation. "Let's make plans and then have a spot of lunch. I'm a bit peckish. I do welcome the coffee." We all kept our eyes on her while she sat back down and took a few sips—and didn't keel over.

I told her about the way I found the bed covers this morning.

"If they can get in to leave wine and fruit salad, maybe coming in the middle of night, we should put bolts on the doors."

Kevin's face went from agog to contemplating the next film—an attempted murder of the P.M. I had to laugh. Looks like I'd be back again next year. But he was thinking something else. "I'll get the crew's carpenter to do that." He pulled out his cell and moved away while talking into it. When he came back to the table, he said. "He'll take care of it."

"Defacing National Trust Property, are you? What's next? Procrastination?" She laughed at her joke. I recognized it as a quote, starting off with murder and ending up with procrastination. Couldn't remember who coined it. Definitely someone English.

Kevin's usually ruddy cheeks drained of color. He started to make another call on his cell, to the carpenter, I guessed.

"Do it," she said. "Lovely idea. We'll feel much safer, won't we?" She reached out and nudged me. I laughed. Kevin's color returned. "All right then. Lunch. I have my walking shoes in here somewhere." She looked in her large bag, pulled out her wig and tugged it on. "Ah, here they are." She kicked off her heels and stepped into flats. "Are we ready?"

We were all slow to react. I wasn't sure what the men were thinking, but it was something, to tell by Kevin's grimace and Peter's almost crossed eyes. I stood and grabbed my daypack that I was using as a purse. I was ready.

"You weren't thinking of eating here at the Stables cafeteria?" Peter asked, almost in a pleading voice.

"Some place we can be waited on, pretend we're jolly tourists. Get a little sunshine. I know just the place," she replied.

The three of us stood at attention while she headed for the stairs. "Sir Walter Raleigh visited here. I'm sure you knew that," she said as she descended the stairs. "A Gilbert owned the property first, built a house, then his son took over. Walter was a half-brother and came here often." As she said the last words I realized it was in the National Trust book on Greenway that I'd briefly reviewed earlier.

Kevin said to me, "Do put that in your script."

"I'm on it," I replied with a grin. And I could add even more with my newfound information. Originally Agatha had bought thirty-eight acres, a much smaller size from the original estate first occupied in the 1500s. Definitely green—a forest down to the River Dart, which curled around the property, walled gardens, Peach House and vinery—it deserved the name 'Greenway.'

Off we went like little ducklings following mama, for in some places on the path we had to walk single file. The P.M. chatted away, talking about the area, nothing political like the unemployment rate, but more about the weather and why the area was called the English Riviera.

"Gilbert bought the property in 1503 and various generations of the family lived here until 1700. His son Humphrey claimed Newfoundland for Queen Elizabeth the First," she told us.

At lunch, the two men finally came out of their catatonic state and were almost their usual amusing selves as they made light jokes. I would say they each weighed their words before speaking. They never did that. Did they think they might be locked up in the Tower of London? Peter was an American citizen, but he straddled both worlds. Kevin was as English as Sticky Toffee Pudding. However, nothing of consequence was said. The P.M. seemed relaxed as her accent changed from BBC to another, but I couldn't identify what area of the country it came from. Kevin could. I'd ask him later.

The P.M. set the tone. Just friends out enjoying each other's company, no serious stuff like how the murder attempts on her were made.

That night we shared the bedroom, but we had our own separate bathrooms. Overhead shower that could be handheld. I had learned from experience that if I dropped it, the water sprayed the room, the shower head landing so that it sprayed me in the face while I tried to pick it up. Those hand-held showers had minds of their own, were alive. Anyhow, the showerhead worked well, good water pressure, that is, it didn't just come out in a trickle. And the water temperature stayed somewhat constant, that is, it didn't vacillate from below freezing to above boiling before I could gasp.

The P.M. had a white cotton, Victorian-style nightgown with a frilly collar that looked like a long housedress. Not that I was Ms. Chic. Mine was a regular silk-imitation, long brown slip-style. We climbed into our individual twins, mine closest to the window, and turned our nightstand lights out. Thankfully no late night talk. Then I remembered the procrastination quote by Thomas Quincey. *"If once a man indulges himself in murder, very soon he comes to think little of robbing; and from robbing he next comes to drinking and sabbath-breaking, and from that to incivility and procrastination.*

That put me fast asleep, no procrastination.

Suddenly—a ferocious barking. If the dog was as big as its bark, I hoped it was on our side.

I went to the window and peered out. A German Shepherd was straining at the leash a man held firmly. "What's happening," I yelled down. The P.M. was at the side of the curtain, not seen from below.

"Got a new watchdog. Think he's after a fox. Know anything about the ladder?"

Ladder? Then I looked. There was a tall extension ladder reaching up to the window of the floor beneath us. "No."

"Workmen must've left it. Sorry to wake you. As I said, have a new dog here, the old one wouldn't have raised such a ruckus. Hip problems."

I guessed the latter comment had to do with the old dog, probably a German Shepherd also if it had hip problems.

"The Curious Incident of the Dog in the Night-time," the P.M. whispered.

"Sherlock Holmes," I said. "Because the watch dog didn't bark in the night."

"That too, but it's a highly successful West End play, going to Los Angeles," the P.M. whispered.

I pulled the curtains closed and went back to bed. The adrenaline had whooshed away as quickly as it had come and I wanted to get my eight hours in. "Morning," I mumbled. As I drifted off, I realized that the person with the ladder probably knew about the new bolt on the door, so they were trying to come in through the window. They didn't have time to extend the ladder one more floor to the room we were in, before the hound of the Baskervilles—in the shape of a German Shepherd—barked. I was mixing up stories—that was my last thought.

In the morning, I called Kevin and told him about the dog and the ladder and to check on the latter. Why was it there? I told him what my suspicions were.

When I took a breath, Kevin said, "Can the P.M. hear you?"

"No," I answered.

"There was an attack on a woman in Leeds last night," he said. "She looks a lot like the P.M."

"Where's Leeds?"

"Not here, that's the good part of the news."

"Did anyone else make that connection?"

"Others," he said. "That's the front page news. Now the P.M. has been sighted all over England, the U.S. and other places. Either she's off having an affair, or having a baby, or she's died and her administrative assistants are trying to cover it up."

"Is this in the news or just in your brain?"

"Doesn't matter. It's the logical deduction. Don't tell her. I don't want to upset her."

Upsetting me was okay though. "Ah, Kevin, just check on the ladder and the dog for now. Toodles," I said in my best British accent, stretching the one word to three.

A knock on the door. I did have a robe on and the kettle was boiling. I was torn whether to pour the boiling water over the English tea leaves or answer the door to a guy who might have a tray of coffee that might be poisoned.

After unbolting the door I didn't even have time to scream. Someone in a monk's outfit, with a skeleton mask, grabbed my throat and starting choking. That swung me into action, and I kneed the figure with every ounce of strength that I had. He tumbled backwards down the stairs. I slammed the door and put the bolt on.

"What was that?" the P.M. asked.

"Someone trying to kill you, only they got me instead." I called Security. Of course, when they asked me to identify the assailant, a little was lost in the translation when I tried to describe the assailant's garb. "Just look for somebody bent over," I said instead of repeating the outfit. Easy for whoever did it to yank off the robe and mask. The dent in his masculinity was another problem.

After the Security people left, I made tea. The P.M. was perking up the coffee, so we sat and exchanged the latest. While sipping, the P.M. said, "I've some papers to go through. Perhaps we can meet back here for lunch." *Was I getting the royal brush off? Being told to leave? Or was she just stating a fact? Why was I cluttering up my head with these pointless thoughts?*

"I've got some research to do, so rendezvousing for lunch sounds great." We went to our separate showers. I still had my clothes in the downstairs bedroom so I changed there, ringing Kevin on his mobile (which is what it's called here). Voice mail. "Hi Kevin. I'm going to the Kwan Yin Pond. Meet me there if you can. I have news. Breaking news," I emphasized, then I picked up my daypack and left.

In the National Trust booklet, it said that over the years the various owners improved the gardens. The Peach House, of course, sheltered growing peaches. I thought about home in California, where everyone who had a back or front yard could have a peach tree—no greenhouse needed.

Down the Middle Path to the Pond where the statue of Kwan Yin, the Goddess of Peace, reigned. The sculpture by Nicholas Dimbleby (I can't make up names like that) was given to the National Trust by the Hicks, Agatha's daughter and son-in-law. I knelt at the edge of the pond to take in the ambiance. So peaceful.

Suddenly I was pushed forward, my face in the water and my head held down. My stunt training kicked in, my reaction automatic— reach up and pull the head of the assailant over my shoulders. Fear made me stronger, and muscle memory remembered the moves.

Splash. A few quick breaths and I ran—full tilt into Kevin.

"What?"

"Quick, we've got to get out of here."

"Let's hide instead." He pulled me off the path and into the bushes where we lay prone, peering out from underneath the branches, my heart thumping against the leaf-covered ground. We didn't talk. Time went by and no one appeared except insect-type critters—plenty of those.

Then we got up, looking like two lovers canoodling in the bushes. We brushed ourselves off. I told him the breaking news of the morning—the appearance of pseudo death's head. And then about my latest encounter.

"Why is someone trying to kill you?"

"They think I'm the P.M. Same hair style, same build. That's all I can come up with."

"I don't see any resemblance."

"Good, that means you're not the attacker."

"Har, har," he said. "The P.M.! She could be in danger."

"Not if they were following me. They don't know there are two of us in the apartment. She said she was going to be looking at papers, and when I came back we could go to lunch."

"Hopefully, no Death's Head on the menu."

Sometimes Kevin's dry humor surprised me. We heard some tromping on the path and stepped aside. Four EMTs dog-trotted past us loaded with equipment and a stretcher. "Injured man in the pond," I thought one of them said.

"Tell me how you did that again?"

"I did some stunt work for the movies. It's on my resume," I said defensively. "Caught him by surprise, otherwise never would have been able to flip him."

"I see," he said, but he didn't look like he did.

"I have to sit down. My adrenaline rush just dissipated." I plopped down on a bench.

The quartet came by at a slower pace, a body on the stretcher, its face covered. Ohoh. "Fell and broke his neck," one of them said as we stared. Then on they went.

I had killed him? While I was feeling terrible, it suddenly occurred to me, it was more like him or me—and the four EMTs could have had my bode on their stretcher. A big sigh of relief. I wasn't ready yet. I still had an informercial to write.

"We have to report this to the police. He was a would-be murderer of the P.M.," Kevin said, watching them until they disappeared from view. "I hope the P.M. is all right."

We climbed the stairs to the third floor of the apartment. No mayhem. The P.M. was sitting at the kitchen table.

"Are we doing lunch?" I asked.

The words were out when I saw that she had a gun trained on us. "Where is she?"

"Where is who?" Kevin asked.

"The Prime Minister, idiot! Where is she?"

"We thought you were the Prime Minister," I said as though that explained everything.

"Well, I'm not! And I want to know where she is." My suite mate was quite miffed.

"We don't know," Kevin said. "There have been two attempts on her life." He pointed at me. "Are you behind that?"

"What?" She looked bewildered, then her face cleared. "So they thought you were the P.M."

"I'm not, and you're not. I have to sit down. I've had rather a strenuous morning." I pulled out a chair and sat. I felt like asking her how her morning was and how her 'papers' were. I guessed she spent part of the time going through my suitcase and my clothes looking for my papers. Well, she would have found a copy of my passport, verifying who I was.

"Who are you?" I asked. "Now that you know who we are and aren't."

"I'm an actress, playing decoy for the P.M. There are about seven of us around the country. Scotland Yard is trying to trap whoever is trying to kill her. Supposedly they were guarding me. Obviously not since you were attacked."

"You're pretending to be the P.M. and you're going to kill her?" I squeaked out the words.

"Of course not." Accent change again. Cockney? I couldn't ask Kevin at the moment. "I'm with a group who just wants to keep her in a safe place until the government gets us back into the EU."

I looked at Kevin for explanation. "EU. European Union. Brexit—ah, that means Britain exit—get out of the European Union. Majority vote of the people not to be a member. Too many foreigners coming in, present American company excepted."

"Now you two, I really must know where the P.M. is."

"We don't know," Kevin said.

"I may have to shoot your kneecap off."

"What!" Kevin turned white.

I'm sure I blanched a little, too, even though it wasn't my kneecap. "He doesn't know and neither do I, so you can shoot us until you run out of bullets. Since we thought you were the P.M., you can see how up to date we are on what she looks like and where she is."

The woman we thought was the P.M. dropped her hand with the gun to her side. "I've got to be the first to find her."

Under other circumstances I would offer to help. If only Agatha or her ghost would make an appearance now. Or write us out of this situation.

Suddenly the door flew open. The pseudo P.M. raised her gun but Kevin pushed the table into her. I dove after her, both of us wrestling for the gun. A shot went off. We looked at each other, the gun was pointed away from both of us. Suddenly the most beautiful German Shepherd in the world had his teeth around our wrists.

"We'll take that now, miss, a brown-suited man said as he twisted the gun away from the three of us. The dog let go first. A woman in uniform helped me up. Kevin said, "Not her, the other one."

Eventually the police straightened out who the good guys were and who wasn't. Much later we learned that the person who tried to kill me was a crazed voter who was mad at the P.M. because she didn't keep all of her promises. The police had his notebook which detailed his frustrations.

The pseudo P.M. was telling the truth—she and her group just wanted to kidnap the P.M, no murder intended. I'd have to come back here for another trial, like I did for the attempted murder and mayhem that occurred last May. Now Kevin had another story he could film here—that of the attempted kidnapping of the P.M.

The big mystery was—would I be able to stay in Agatha Christie's apartment again?

~The End~

GREENWAY REVISITED
A mystery short story

Kevin, our London producer, prepared to do some heavy negotiating with the National Trust folk. This would be our third film on Greenway and there had been a few mishaps in the way of dead bodies. Real ones, not reel ones and that was the problem. Christie-like, perhaps, but not National Trust-like. Kevin understood that the Trust wasn't enamored of the unnaturally deceased on the property, no matter that there were several in the Agatha Christie books that resided in the house she had owned. Kevin was up to the task, but he had to put a spin on his spiel, because money wouldn't work. He could say that the film crew added to the economy in the area—but tourists did that also and there were plenty of those.

We were now filming the documentary of the attempted murders on the Greenway property and the real murders elsewhere by the same person. The National Trust worried, primarily, about how the murders would affect Greenway's reputation. Also, they were worried about this documentary, which was the story of the two attempts on my life, and on a sort of P.M. involvement. (P.M. standing for Prime Minister.) After all, the P.M. was the head of the National Trust in a way, as she was the head of the government—after the Queen, of course. And—what would the Queen think? That was the P.R. mess that Kevin waded into.

He told me to continue with the script I was writing. Write on! I had moved out of Greenway to Dartmouth, a short ferry or train ride away, and was staying on the top floor at the Dartmouth Railway Inn. The ceiling slanted over the bed, creating the coziness of an attic room which was so cute that I was ready to move in permanently. Alas, no Agatha Christie vibes here, more of a Jane Austen atmosphere, with the Wedgewood blue and white—not the miasma I needed for my script. Ah, well.

The room was newly refurbished with a lingering smell of paint. The floor was uneven, maybe because the building was about three hundred years old. No other sign of age in the room. Because of the slight tilt, or maybe because of a poltergeist, the bathroom door slowly swung shut with a click. I had to remember to close it, otherwise I'd be constantly scared silly. The first time I had turned around I was staring at another person, nude, the light from the window turning the figure into a silhouette. My heart flip-flopped trying to find a place to hide, just as I realized it was my reflection in the mirror on the back of the door. Death by mirror.

The script I was writing gave the details of the encounter last May, a year ago, when I almost joined my ancestors. That had encouraged me to increase my exercises. Assiduously I was now doing the extreme regime I'd been taught during my brief stint in stunt school. I'd been exercising to keep limber, using all of my muscles, but now I strengthened those I would need for any serious confrontation. Not that I expected any, but I'd met two separate would-be assailants over the past year, so what were my chances?

Sitting at the small desk in front of the window in my room, a window through which I stared over the myriad of rooftops and chimney pots, I contemplated how many different kinds and shapes of both there were. That meant I was not keyboarding. I had to go back to Greenway, preferably to the holiday apartment, but that wasn't going to happen. It was full of other holidayers, or as they would say here—holiday makers.

In the breakfast room, Kevin sat down at my small table. "…ahhh, I need a favor." He would spell it 'favour,' I thought, then realized he was waiting for me to say 'yes' or 'what?' and I waited for him to go on. He looked a little nervous compared to his usual implacability.

"Okay, hit me."

"What? I wouldn't hit you."

"Kevin, it's an Americanism. Hit me with the info about what you want."

"Oh, ahhh…my sister…can you spend some time with her. Take her—"

"Kevin. I have a script to write. Two weeks you gave me. That's when the crew is going to start filming. Plus dear director Peter wants me available every breathing second he's directing in case he needs a script change. I have no time to spend with anyone else, even though, I'm sure your sister is as charming as you." Would that get me off the hook?

"She's not."

"Not—your sister?"

"Not charming. In fact, that's the problem, she's as lacking in charm as anyone can be."

"Kev, dear heart, I'm missing something here."

"Missing? What did you lose?"

Sigh. "Another Americanism. Why do you want me to spend time with your sister if she isn't charming? What else is wrong with her?"

"Let me count the ways." He put a hand to his forehead in a pseudo-dramatic way. Not Kevinish at all.

"Spill the beans."

46

"I do know what that means." He smiled, but it quickly vanished. "Just have dinner with us tonight." He was about to add more, but he closed his mouth, compressing his lips.

"Your shout?" I knew he'd understand that Britishism, although I think that was only used in pubs.

He nodded, but with obvious reluctance. "We'll meet you here in the lobby at 7. It's just a short walk. At least she'll have someone else to talk to besides me."

"Okeydokey."

"What?"

I waved as I left the breakfast room to closet myself for a while and knock out some pages. Then I wanted to visit Greenway's developed gardens, but not the Kwan Yin Pond—she was not a peaceful goddess for me anymore. And why would be in the script.

Dartmouth was a busy town, particularly in the summer. The area was called the English Rivera, because of the mild climate, so it became a popular destination for holidayers. Ferries went up and down the River Dart, making it an easy way to get to Greenway, Agatha Christie's holiday home. If I had to be on location anywhere, that mode of transportation, gliding past the lovely scenery, was at the top of my list. Of course, hanging around her property wasn't bad either.

At 7, Kevin and I were in the small lobby of the Dartmouth Railway Inn. "Tell me more about your sister," I said to forestall any questions about how I was progressing on the script. I knew he wanted it yesterday—but that fast, I didn't write. In fact, I was stalled. "There she is now."

Sis had orange hair. Think it was supposed to be reddish, but loving hands at home doing the coloring process missed the correct hue. Or maybe that's what she wanted. It was short, just covering her ears.

47

The bangs, or rather the fringe, followed the curve of her forehead, so they were higher in the middle than on the sides.

She immediately started talking. "I don't know why we have to eat so late. At home it's 5 on the dot."

Kevin introduced us, but I was as noticeable as a flea. Her hand just slid off mine, no intention of a grip, nor any interest. We both looked at Kevin for our next instruction.

"I thought we'd go to an Italian restaurant—"

"Kevin." Actually she said his name as if she was holding her nose and speaking. "You know I can't eat tomato sauce. It's too acidic and it…"

I tuned out, looked away, maybe even backed up a few steps as she went on to describe the journey of the tomato sauce down her gullet and through the various passages then out. I'll never have anything with tomato sauce on it ever again.

Kevin appeared stunned at first—and she was only at her diaphragm, then he kept trying to interrupt her, talking about other things on the menu. Those without the dreaded T.S., as I now mentally referred to the offending tomato sauce. I checked my phone. Dang, no texts or emails, not even spam or an ad. She was an orange-headed doll that had been wound up to give that speech.

Finally, we were on our way. It was a short distance, as Kevin had said. Ensconced at a table, I considered ordering a bottle of Scotch, skip the glass, but since I didn't drink anymore, it had to be a bottle of something milder. We perused the menu. I debated about something heavy on the T.S., with a side of it, but opted for an innocuous salad. Madame Orange ordered fettuccine alfredo. Kevin had an order of knives—whoops—I mean eggplant. When the waiter took our order, would you believe, Madame Orange started to go through her digestive digression. I had a sudden urge to visit the ladies room to make an

48

inventory of what was in my purse—so I did that. I timed her, then went back to join the compatible brother and sister duo. Kevin's eyes looked a little crossed. Not really, but I'm sure they wanted to look at each other instead.

"Where is the loo?" Before I could give her directions, she said, "I've got a bladder infection—"

At that point I fainted. No, but I felt like it. Instead I knocked over a glass of water. Kevin and I both scrambled to mop it up while she faded into the background muttering something about a gynecologist.

"I know, I know, but I've got to get somebody to be with her. Her husband's looking for her."

"Why?" It was an honest question

"It's got to do with their divorce. Umm…he's...umm…threatened her."

I sat stunned for moment. "Kevin, you gave me a long speech about not getting involved with any more murderers anywhere near Greenway, and now you want me to spend time with a woman whose husband—"

My voice must have been rising, because Kevin looked around and leaned across the table whispering, "She's back."

I gripped my purse ready for another run to the ladies' room in case she was going to change channels to another depressing speech.

"The water's not very hot in there. My allergy doctor says to wash my hands in hot soapy water, not tepid. The germs proliferate, particularly on my skin because—"

The waiter was setting our plates down carefully on the table. Since none of us had ordered anything with T.S. on it, no mix-up. He left quickly, not asking if we wanted anything else.

She ate like a pig. She circled her arm around her plate, hunched over and attacked it with a fork. Strands of spaghetti flopped savagely every which way. I got a few globs and so did Kevin. Luckily it was white sauce. I was so mesmerized by her behavior that I almost forgot to eat. She was sitting beside me at the table for four. I didn't dare look at Kevin.

Occasionally she looked up and stared straight ahead as she ate the last of the pasta. She seemed fascinated by what she was looking at. I had to lean slightly toward her to see there was a mirror on the wall directly in front of her. She made faces in it, not dramatically so, but twitches, turning her head slightly side to side. Luckily, I only had Kevin to look at.

After she had eaten, she stood up. Neither Kevin and I were finished. "I'm going back to the Inn," she said. And left. I think she belched on the way, but I could be mistaken.

We finished, ordered coffee and chatted. Kevin was fidgety. Not a good sign.

"I hate to ask this, but could she stay the night with you?"

Incredulity was my first reaction. But I answered like an adult. "I only have a twin bed, my room is the size of a closet, so no." I was frantically thinking about how I could dismantle the other twin bed and hide it.

"Then, stay in her room."

"I think not," I said in my most haughtily queenly manner. "*You* stay in her room."

"What! What if her husband burst in there in the middle of the night and shot me because he thought I was her lover?"

"What if he thought your sister had become a lesbian and I was her lover?"

"Hmmm," Kevin sagely hummed.

"I'm appalled that you are putting me into so much danger. Speaking of shooting. He has a gun?"

"Ah...well...maybe several."

"Lovely. Here we are a dart's throw from Agatha Christie's property and an arsenal is about to appear gunning for us. The National Trust will not be amused."

Kevin looked away, as though off in the distance was the perfect caregiver riding up on a white steed.

"Can't you come up with someone else to play minder? How about a Sumo wrestler?"

"She likes you."

Jaw dropping time. I wasn't going to ask how he came to that conclusion, although I was curious. "She likes my ears—all she wants is something to talk into, unload on... Wait, speaking of guns, does she have one?"

"For protection."

"There you are—the perfect bedmate."

"What if I offered you a cash bonus?"

'You can offer me the Taj Mahal, I ain't bitin'."

He nodded. He's been in too many negotiating sessions not to know when it's over, it's over.

"Has her husband actually tried to kill her?" I almost whispered this.

"I don't know. I only know she left because she thought he might try to kill her. They are going through a rough divorce."

I didn't waste any brain power imaging that scenario. "If you want my advice, Kevin, stay out of it. Your sister can take care of herself. And you don't have a gun. Besides, how do we know she's telling the truth—or what the truth is?"

"Actually, she's my half-sister. I only just met her. She said our father had two families, but she was the only child."

"You didn't know about her before? Kevin, this sounds like a giant scam. Do you have any proof? Get a blood test and you'll know for sure. You're being used. There's no way that woman could be related to you in any way."

"I thought of that, but I didn't want to hurt her feelings."

"She's a scam artist and she's using you. Cut her off."

"But what about her husband? What if he harms her?"

I didn't answer that question with *then she'll be out of your life.* Instead I said, "Walk away while you still have your life and your wallet."

When I climbed into bed, I prayed with more enthusiasm than I ever had before that I would soon be delivered from this situation.

"Help me, help me!"

I froze in my bed. Wide awake. This was no dream. There was a pounding on the door of the room next to mine—only two rooms on this floor. No one was in there that I knew of. More pounding. Madame. Orange for sure, but I wasn't going out there. She was looking for me and had the wrong room number, unless she was just pounding on doors at random. I wondered what she wanted help from, but I wasn't going to try to find out. I had no remorse about not opening the door and being deluged with words of ailments. If I had a gun I'd shoot myself first. She needed more help than I could ever give her.

Then, I hear Kevin's voice. He sounded soothing, leading her away, down the stairs. Was she sleep walking? Drunk? Or is she on her way to Bedlam? Whatever. Looney tunes is looney tunes.

Why didn't she go to Kevin's room first? Maybe she did and didn't wait for him to come to the door. Maybe he was coming to warn me and found her.

Maybe I just dreamed the whole thing. Too bad I can't put this into my script, pad it a little, hype up the suspense. But, it didn't happen in Agatha Christie's holiday apartment—and that was where the script had to be set.

The next day I hit the keyboard first thing, foregoing morning tea. I stayed in my jammies, not feeling like getting ready for the world. I had to write some pages, this was not a holiday for me, nor even a working vacation. Delete the word 'vacation.'

That meant by lunchtime I was ready to eat an entire buffet. I made my way to the closest restaurant and as I was pursuing the menu thinking about having one of everything—Madame Orange plopped down. Astonishment, not to mention other emotions, like horror, struck me. I thought of pretending I'd already eaten and scurry out, but I didn't. Curiosity, an ailment of writers, took hold. Was she really a scam artist who glommed onto Kevin for some reason?

Lunch was palatable. In fact, she didn't say much while she ate. And she didn't need a trough, but then it was a sandwich that didn't drip. I was figuratively holding my breath. Hard to eat that way. Luckily I had nothing with the dreaded T.S. on it—linguini with clams that was drippy. I was the one who needed a trough.

She talked like a normal person. I asked her a few questions about Kevin and she told me the same story he had about how she had found him.

"We have the same last name, and I remembered my father—our father—saying he had a son named Kevin. I asked him about that and his words were, 'If I had a son, I'd name him Kevin.' But I know that's not what he said the first time."

I asked her a few more questions. But wasn't any more enlightened about their supposed joint father. She was off-subject, or else being evasive in her answers. I thought the latter.

The waiter put our bills for lunch on the table. She said, "Thank you for lunch."

I leaned forward and practically hissed, "I'm not buying you lunch, honey, here's your bill."

"Let me buy," she said, and snatched up both bills. Now I felt badly. The woman never ceased to amaze me. I snatched mine back. "Thanks, anyway. Appreciate the thought." I tried to smile, but only bared my teeth.

After we left the money with our bills, I stood up to leave. She started talking about the area and the weather—nothing negative or medicinal. She opened the large bag she used as a purse and sifted around in it, then came up with case for her glasses, folding them carefully into it. Then she *placed*—YES!—the case into the satchel. That was the only way to describe the size of the bag. From where I was standing the innards looked jumbled. I started to move away, but she wasn't finished. She rummaged around some more, came up with another glasses case, and slowly took out sunglasses, still talking and pausing to look at me. Then she placed that case on the top of the pile, closed the bag.

Ah, now I can go. But no. She stood up and took her jacket, carefully, off the back of the chair, and slowly put it on. Now?

No! She began to button it up. There were a *lot* of tiny buttons. I didn't remember it being buttoned up when she first sat down. But I was in a state of horror at the time. She had her sunglasses on and was trying to match buttonhole up with button. Obviously she couldn't see that well in her now-darkened environment. Not to mention that it was warm out and a jacket was not needed. I didn't say anything about that—not that I could get a word in—as she might regale me with her anemic blood condition.

"I'm off," I said. "Have to dash to Greenway."

"Wait."

But I didn't, pretending not to hear her, I waved goodbye. With luck, I'd catch the ferry and she'd miss it. But that was not to be. I was in line for the ferry so she caught up with me. Dang.

"I wanted to tell you that I'm related to Agatha Christie."

Just like you're related to Kevin, I thought. "Really? Tell me all about it."

"It's her mother's family—Miller. My mother was a Miller and she's a cousin."

"You mean your mother was a cousin of Agatha's father, not her mother?" Did I sound monumentally doubtful?

"That's right!" She said it as though I guessed the correct answer.

"She was the daughter of which brother?" Agatha's father didn't have any brothers.

She didn't answer, instead diverting my attention to pointing out that Kevin was at the dock. Then she waved good-bye to me, or maybe it was tallyho.

They didn't share the same mother so he wouldn't be related to Agatha, even distantly. I was even more convinced now that she was a scam artist taking advantage of poor Kevin. Couldn't believe the man was so gullible.

The two of us and a few other people boarded a different ferry, took us almost stone's throw distance across the River Dart. Kevin led me to the historic little railway station so that we could take the train on a short ride to Greenway. I hardly noticed because we were so deep in conversation.

"I'm getting the actors for the script you're working on. Peter wants to play himself. What about you?" he asked.

"Playing myself? No, thanks. I'm not an actor. Besides you have someone cast already in the documentary Peter is filming now. Continuity and all that. The three films are really a series—the first one the documentary on the history of Greenway, and the second one about the murders that happened while we were filming the documentary. And now this one, the third one, about our encounter with a famous person. What about you? Are you going to play yourself?"

"No one asked."

"What do you want to do?" I asked, as we climbed aboard. At the station was a small museum about the railroad's history. Thomas Newcomen was born in Dartmouth, and it was claimed he was the inventor of the world's first steam engine—we were traveling on his progeny. We rode it to the Greenway stop, which was called, fittingly enough, *Greenway Halt*, got off and walked to the main house.

'By the way, I ran into your sister. She says she's related to Agatha Christie." I tried to keep the disbelief out of my voice.

"On her mother's side, so I'm not related. We shared fathers."

"Shared fathers? Do you think it's true?"

"Could be. That's why she came here."

Double scam. Maybe triple. "Is she planning on contacting her Agatha relatives?"

He shrugged.

Since he wasn't going to say anymore on that subject, I asked, "Are we going to be able to get into the apartment to film the script I'm working on?"

"I'm negotiating that. We're not going to have a lot of time in there. Peter said he'd shoot the interior here and then when he gets back to the studio in California, add what he has to."

The script Peter was filming was set place in Agatha Christie's holiday apartment. High possibility we would be banned from the grounds altogether, since we had attracted murder and mayhem in our first two projects on the property.

Today, the crew was working down by the Boathouse where the actual denouement had taken place during the first filming. The sightseers were kept at bay until 3 p.m. Even though there were enough other sights to see on the Greenway grounds, a look at *the* Boathouse, the scene of the crime in *Dead Man's Folly,* in Agatha Christie's short story, was a big draw here.

Our conversation was interrupted by a man on the path who was making a bit of a ruckus with the film set's guard. Kevin went over and I sidled close enough to listen, but not participate.

"My missus is here and I've come to fetch her home."

"Who is that?" Kevin asked.

The man said the name. Kevin's sister! This was the would-be murderer of Madame Orange? He sure didn't look the part—but what murderer did, except in a mug shot at the police department.

"Said she had a part in some TV series here."

Ah ha! Another one of her lies.

"No one in the crew with that name," Kevin said. That was the truth.

"Got to get her back. Rent's due and she's got the checkbook. It's all in her name, too."

Interesting. Was she the wage earner? Also interesting that he only wanted her back to sign checks—or rather, cheques, as it is spelled here. Or maybe that was a ruse to find her, particularly if he had murder in his eye and a gun in his pocket.

"Can't help you, sir." Kevin said, turning away, probably hoping the man would also.

"Who's in charge here?" His voice became belligerent. Had he been drinking? He had the signs of one—broken blood vessels in his face.

"Actually, I am," Kevin said. That was the truth also.

"What's your name?" he pulled out a wrinkled piece of paper and the stub of a pencil. Was he for real?

"Think you'd better move on, sir, you're in the wrong place." This from the guard. "You can ask at the National Trust office. It's—"

"Been there. They sent me here. I want some satisfaction. I want to know where my missus is."

Apparently the guard had not been idle, for down the path came a National Trust vehicle—golf cart type—with two National Trust security people in it. Not burly Commando-types, but two Irish lassie-types. I had no doubt they could handle him if it came to rough-and-tumble stuff, but they were all smiles. Diplomacy at its best. "Come and have a cuppa with us and then we can sort this all out. Let's see if we can get you quickly reunited with your wife," the driver said.

It worked. Docilely, or rather mesmerized by their smiles, or maybe he liked lovely lasses in polo-and-shorts uniforms, he climbed onto their chariot in a daze and off they went.

Kevin turned to the guard. "Thanks, Stuart." Kevin knew everyone—after all, he had hired them.

Stuart responded, "We always make friends with the local constabulary. In this case, the National Trust security—and a pleasure it's been. Fiona and Kelly—they're the best. Wouldn't want to be on the wrong side of either of them any day of the week."

Kevin nodded. "Carry on." We moved away.

"Your sister," I whispered.

He nodded. "Caught me by surprise."

"You looked stoic—but then you always do."

"Have to in this business. Can't give away how I really feel."

"What now?"

"Let my sister know he's here. And let her decide what to do. If she doesn't pay the rent on their flat—assuming he's telling the truth—she's not going to have a home."

"Speaking of telling the truth—do you think your sister is really your sister, or half-sister? She could just be saying that to hit you up for money."

"My dad was with us during the week, and then on the weekends he was traveling for his job. She told me it was the opposite with her. She said her dad—our dad—was with them on the week-ends then traveling during the week."

I gasped at that. "I can see why you believe her. Does she have any other proof? Letters he wrote? Pictures? Anything?"

"Just taking it one day at a time. See what she's up to."

"She lied to her husband about having a part in a TV series—"

"Maybe just to get away. A promise of more money."

I clamped my mouth shut. None of my business. I was looking at this like it was a TV script and I was responsible for coming up with motivation and the next action. Not so.

We took the ferry back to the Inn. One of the perks of staying here—and I can understand why Agatha Christie loved it so much—cool breezes where we sat outside on the ferry, ogling the lovely scenery sailing by. Suspended animation—not having to do anything, floating peacefully to our destination. We didn't talk, too much to look at and enjoy.

At the Inn, Madame Orange had just arrived, also from whatever expedition she'd been on. Kevin took her elbow and guided her into the bar lounge. I went along out of sheer nosiness. No one said I couldn't. We ordered soft drinks from the bartender. No wait person here. Tray in hand, Kevin sat down at a corner table with comfy padded swivel chairs.

He told her about hubby looking for his missus.

"He found me," she said. But she didn't seem too upset, only annoyed. "I knew he would, but I didn't expect him so soon."

"You told him where you were going—working on a TV series. It wouldn't be hard to find you—we're the only film crew in the area."

Neither of them had much of a reaction. To me, it was a no-brainer, if she told him where she was going—why was she miffed he had found her so soon? Guy probably wanted his egg and chips at dinner and discovered they didn't appear magically on the table when she wasn't there. I didn't understand this family—if that's what they were.

When Kevin mentioned about the rent money, she said, "He has money. He's probably using it here for a hotel room." She said this in a matter-of-fact manner.

Where was all the fear he was going to kill her? She seemed as unperturbed as Kevin usually looked.

"What are you going to do?" Kevin asked. It was what I wanted to know also.

"Go back with him, I guess. To my boring life. I'm tired of doing the same things all the time. And he wants the same things to eat all the time At the same time. It's too much." She was so animated in her protestations. Like a doll wound up.

Kevin said nothing. Just took a few sips of his drink.

"Can't you hire me?" she asked. "I'll be somebody's dogsbody, but I can't go back to that humdrum life and that dismal flat. It's dark and it's either too hot or too cold. Stanley is so boring."

If her life was so boring, had she invented the story that her husband was trying to kill her? Invented the Kevin relationship—and best of all, the Agatha relatives? Maybe Stanley was trying to kill her—but with boredom, not the gun he supposedly had. I almost guffawed, but coughed instead.

Kevin stood up. "I've got some work to do. See you in the morning."

I jettisoned myself out of the comfy padded chair. No way was I staying.

We left, leaving her with three unfinished drinks, as though she hadn't noticed. I imagined her finishing them all off for something different to do.

As we climbed the stairs to the second floor where Kevin's room was, I said, "I thought her husband was trying to kill her."

"Maybe she exaggerated."

"He's a clod. He wouldn't kill a weed, let alone shoot anybody with one of his many guns—if he has any."

Kevin didn't say anything, just walked to his room. I continued to the third floor which was up two more flights. At least they were short ones.

I felt I'd just fallen asleep when there was a knock on my door and my name whispered. Kevin. I touched the light on my travel clock. 2:29. I pulled on my cotton wrap-around robe and tied the sash while I answered him. A moment later I opened the door. He was dressed. "My sister's missing."

I'm not a jump-out-of-bed-wide-awake person, so it took a few seconds to assimilate the information. Then to censor a few sarcastic remarks. Kevin looked concerned.

A crashing sound from the room next door.

Kevin practically jumped the few steps to it and opened the door. It looked like a man and a woman were struggling. The woman fell and the man dove out of the window onto the roof top. I stood at the door while Kevin went to the woman.

Then he switched a lamp on. I thought the room had been empty.

I saw the orange hair and knew whose body it was. With a knife under her left breast—right into her heart, I'm sure. I stood frozen in the doorway. Several thoughts racing through my now-awake mind..

The other thought was that this was the same rooftop that ran under my window—which had been open. I didn't realize someone could come in that way. I thought I was safe, here among the rooftops and chimney pots. What if I was the target? I had been in the past.

"She's dead. Call the desk from your room. I'll stay here."

I backed out and did as he asked. Then got dressed. Only moments later there were running footsteps up the stairs.

The National Trust would be very happy they had kicked us off the property. But the Inn wouldn't be because they hadn't.

Why had she changed rooms? And right next to mine. Why had she come up the other night knocking on that door, saying, 'Help me, help me'? I thought she had been looking for my room, but maybe it was the person in that room. Who had been staying there? A man? The man who climbed out of the window? Why would he stab her? A thief who was trying to steal something while she slept?

What if she changed rooms to be with him? Maybe he was the real reason she came down here.

Then why did she tell her husband where she was going to be? To make him jealous? If he had attempted to kill her before, wouldn't this be the *coup de grace*?

The next day, the Inn asked us to leave—just Kevin and me, not the rest of the film crew. They weren't dead body magnets. The Inn was very nice about it, refunded last night's scare stay. They didn't offer to get us reservations elsewhere. Now we were on the street with our suitcases. Actually we were in a taxi paid for by the Inn ready to take us wherever we wanted to go. Peter was with us but he hadn't been ousted.

Luckily, Kevin knew the area and if word hadn't spread about our Typhoid Mary personalities, he had booked accommodations in the town where the historical railway that he liked so much, was located. We could still take the train to Greenway Halt. Although I enjoyed the ferry ride, but the train was quicker.

We wondered where Stanley was—if the police were discussing his missus with him. Poor Stanley. He was permanently out of his eggs-and-chips dinner. With luck, he'd find another missus. Maybe one more accommodating.

We had been questioned up one side and down the other until dawn. No one mentioned last year's attempted murders, so they hadn't made the connection.

I was a little numb at this point, low on sleep and caffeine, adrenaline rush long gone. Did this mean another documentary for Kevin? The Inn would never let us film there. I was ready for newer, safer digs after discovering that anyone could hop through the window from the rooftop. I thought about Poe's perpetrator in *Murders in the Rue Morgue*.

"Kevin, do you have any idea why she was stabbed?"

"None. I didn't know her, she'd just come into my life. Like Stanley. I didn't know anything about him. She didn't tell me much, except about my father."

"You believed her." I said it as a statement. I was still incredulous about that.

"She said all the right things. No reason not to believe her. She never asked for anything. I just went along that she was who she said she was."

I gave up trying to find out why he bought into Madame Orange's story. "We know that guy we saw in the room wasn't Stanley, but I wonder who he was. Why were they meeting in that room? Why not her other room?" I'd been asked all those questions. They were my questions also. I didn't have any answers, not even conjectures. Unfortunately, neither did Kevin. "Sorry, musing out loud."

"Might just as well. Talk all you want. We're no further ahead than we were when we saw it happen."

"Yeah, that was pretty spooky, and it wasn't even Halloween."

Kevin gave me a quizzical look but said nothing. Then we were there—at our new home for the next two weeks or so—or until another eviction. Hopefully, not another murder. We checked in, but didn't get to our rooms, although we had our keys. The police wanted to talk to us again, and we were kindly given a lounge area room, set aside for private tete-a-tetes, only with glass all around. No hanky panky here.

The officer gave his card to Kevin and introduced himself— Sergeant Timothy Halstead. "We are at the enquiry stage now," he said. He showed us some pictures of several young men and asked if we recognized any of them. We didn't. Then he gave us a list of names and asked the same question. We gave him the same answer.

I asked about Stanley. Yes, they had interviewed him, and he'd gone back to London. "Which brings up another point. It seems that the victim was dead about six hours give or take, when you saw the man you thought stabbed her."

"What! But I saw—" and then I thought—what did I see? "I thought she was struggling with him, but her arms flopped rather than trying to strike him. She was dead at that point? What was he doing?"

"We've been able to identify him. He thought she had fainted, so he picked her up—then he saw the knife. The light wasn't on, so only moonlight. Then when you two came in, he thought the murderers were coming back for the body."

"You've talked to him?" Kevin asked.

"Yes. He admits he was using the room and that he came in through the window, but he denies knowing who she was or why she was in that room."

"So Stanley's not off the hook, after all."

"We are continuing to investigate," he said rather stiffly, as though teaching a class.

"Do you believe him?"

"We don't disbelieve him, but we can't prove it either way. We have no evidence that directly connects him to the murder. The Inn is completely baffled that someone was in that room. They keep it available in case a VIP shows up unexpectedly."

"There's one other thing we should tell you." I related the 'Help me, Help me' episode. Then Kevin told his part of the story, which I didn't know, about how he heard her leaving in the middle of the night. His room was next to hers. He hurriedly dressed and went after her. He thought she was sleepwalking.

I didn't think so. She was either looking for me, or knew the man was in that room. But I didn't say anything. My thoughts were conjectures only, tainted with annoyance at her while she was alive.

I opened the door to my new digs, took one look at the lovely brand new blonde furniture, red pegs on the wall and closed the door. No table, no desk—and if I saw everything—no closet. I knocked on Kevin's door. "I can't write here—too sterile. I'm going to Greenway."

He didn't say anything, just walked out and closed the door. "I'm going there, too."

"I'll hang out at the Stables Cafe, use one their tables. That way Peter can get me if he wants to change anything." I could write there, I was sure.

We walked the short distance to the train station. Kevin bought our tickets and we were off. If he could purr, I'm sure he would. He loved that historic train. Maybe it was the one he never had as a kid.

The Stables housed a tiny café, and next to it, a lovely shop. At an outdoor table with tea at the ready, my laptop opened, I continued with the script. Visitors swarmed in and out, kids and dogs ran around. None of that bothered me. I was in my own world and could tune them out and concentrate.

This was to be my lucky day, for Officer or Chief Inspector or whatever his title was—Kevin had told but I'd forgotten—Halstead, who had spoken with us at the hotel earlier, said, "May I join you?" I had to come out of my script world, let my eyes focus on him before I could agree. I felt like shaking my head to get back to the moment, shake off the other world, so immersed had I been.

A little chitchat on his part, then he said, "I'd like to ask you a few questions about your friend, Kevin."

"He's not my friend, he's the producer, we work together." I quickly realized how that sounded. "I mean, he is a friend now, but we don't visit back and forth, like friends do. It's a friendly working relationship." I pictured myself at that moment babbling away.

"The reason I'd like to discuss him is that the victim was his sister. And you were also acquainted with her."

A big mental sigh. I nodded. The thought I had earlier popped into my mind. *Husbands and significant others are always the prime suspect.* I gasped and shook my head. "Not Kevin," I said.

"We're looking at everything. I just want to go over a few things."

I could see why they wanted to know more about how we came to go into the room next to mine. If there had been no sound, what reason would Kevin have to open the door, with me as a witness that his sister was already dead? That was the essence of the officer's questioning. Too much of a coincidence. He didn't say that but inferred Kevin could have stabbed her earlier and then 'we' discovered the body together. My thought was that Kevin would know that the autopsy would show she had died earlier, so what good was I as a witness? The officer intimated that the fact we were together when we discovered the body had been engineered by Kevin.

Then my other thought was that another officer was with Kevin intimating that I had killed her and engineered that we discover the body together.

Or that together we had murdered her.

"What about Stanley?" It sounded like I was trying to deflect questions from me. Not that I could picture him as a murderer. Too much interested in keeping his chef and chief check writer alive. Or was that all an act on his part? I doubted it.

"Of course, we are talking to the victim's husband also."

He asked me some more questions and I answered truthfully. I wanted to protest that there was no way Kevin would have killed his half-sister, but I didn't. My protestations wouldn't mean anything.

I felt sick after the officer left. Especially after he asked me what Kevin was wearing when we found the body, exactly what did he touch? Kevin had asked me to have the desk call the police so I didn't know what he did when I left the doorway of the room. What could he do? I didn't go back after I called. Kevin handled everything with the hotel staff until the police came and that's when I came out of my room.

I sat in the swirl of humanity at the Stables when the officer left. My script world disrupted, overturned by the new vision of reliving finding the body. I put everything in my backpack and decided to walk around. All the greenery would help calm me, I hoped. I headed toward where Peter was filming, still at the Boathouse, the story of the murders that occurred on our first visit to make the documentary of Greenway. Remembering all that had the opposite effect—more turmoil. But a different kind. The crew was having lunch, so I settled in to join them, to talk about other things. Greenway wasn't calming me the way it had Agatha.

Everything was going well with Peter, except for the usual minor glitches when nature didn't cooperate, or got too noisy or felt its territory was being invaded.

Later, back at another table at the Stables outside, Kevin appeared with coffee in hand. He looked a little embarrassed. I said, "Did an officer question you alone?" He nodded. "Did he intimate that I killed your sister?'

Kevin hardly looked up, staring into his coffee. "Let me tell you that I had one who intimated you killed her. That means we are both suspects," I said.

"Never!" His wide eyes locked onto mine. "That's preposterous!"

As he took a breath, I said. "Or that we did it together."

"Impossible."

"The moral of the story is never to discover a body. The first on the scene is a suspect," I said.

"Why would we kill her?"

"That doesn't matter at the moment. We had the ability and the proximity. They'll find a motive. Maybe we didn't like orange hair/"

"Out of the question," Kevin said.

Did he mean he liked her neon hair?

People were walking around, pushing strollers, wheel chairs, all quite normal. And here we were on the brink of being accused of a heinous crime. It was almost laughable. In fact it was, so I laughed, Kevin looked startled, wiping away his worried look. I told him what I had been thinking.

"Bet they didn't take your shoes." He looked a little smug, then took a sip of coffee.

I sat back in surprise. "My shoes?"

"Both pairs. Had to go out and buy new ones." He stuck a foot out. A black sock under brown leather sandals.

"They're you. Just like Christ's footwear, but he didn't wear socks."

"I am Jewish, so there could be a resemblance." A big smirk on his face. "Socks are to keep my feet warm and protect them from things that bite here in the wilds."

He sipped coffee for a few minutes. I wanted to get back to the script, but I sensed he wanted to talk. "She had three letters signed with an 'A' addressed to a Mrs. Miller in London."

"That was Agatha's birth name, but you knew that. Who Miller?"

"Don't know."

"Stolen?"

"Don't know that either. The officers asked me about the letters, but didn't give me any details."

"What do you think about her being related to Agatha Christie?" I tried to keep the derision out of my inflection. Didn't succeed.

Kevin shrugged. "It is possible."

Halstead had a female officer with him this time. She gave me her card. Ann Chamberlaine. She was a PCSO—Police Community Support Officer. Did he feel there was more information to get out of me and she would be able to do that? A floating thought as they sat, and he explained about the letters as she pulled them out of her briefcase. They were in large plastic envelopes, but only the envelope containing the letter was in each one. I quickly saved my document and moved my laptop giving them room to spread them out. Obviously we couldn't take them out of the plastic, only view both sides of the envelopes. I picked one up, turned it over. On the back of the envelope was imprinted the address of Greenway. The postmark was smudged. They were addressed only to Mrs. Miller, no first name, and an address in London. I looked at all three. "What's in the letters?"

Halstead nodded to the woman as though giving her permission to answer. "News of the area, of mutual acquaintances, presumably, as only first names are mentioned, such as 'George visited last week.' Chatty, not formal."

"No first name for Mrs. Miller?" I asked.

"Correct. The salutation is 'Dear Cousin,' and signed only with the letter 'A.' Typewritten, probably from a machine made in the 1940s, no later."

"Does the 'A' writing matches Agatha's handwriting?"

"Could be. We haven't done a detailed analysis, as we're still in the preliminary stages," she said. "We want to know if either of you have any information about the letters."

Kevin and I shook our heads.

"Do you think she was killed for the letters?" I asked.

"We found only these three. We don't know if she had others with her."

She didn't answer my question, but I knew there were things they couldn't reveal—even if they knew them. "Did you find out if she was a distant relative of Agatha's?" I asked.

"We're still working on that information,' Halstead said.

They had run out of questions for the time being. Halstead and Chamberlaine left together and Kevin fled in the opposite direction. I got back to work, however my mind wandered to Madame Orange. I searched my memory for anything she might have said or did that referred to the letters. Nada.

What about the man we saw holding her dead body like a rag doll? Did she know he was using that room? I didn't think, now, he was the innocent who happened to be squatting in the Inn's VIP room. It was too unbelievable that the Inn's staff didn't know. Maybe he left no trace.

Maybe the maid or whoever cleaned only came in before a VIP was scheduled to arrive. And why had she wandered up there the previous night asking for help? Sleepwalking or on drugs? Whatever—she was a night too early for her rendezvous with the roof hopper.

The thought of trying to solve a mystery thrilled me. Then reality set in. I didn't have time. I had to finish the script. I was sure Kevin would have suggestions for changes, which would involve more time.

If I had a few spare moments I could pump one of the docents I knew from last year. Before I could run mentally through the list—and as though my thoughts had conjured them up—there were two of them, Ethel and Nora, holding cups of tea and looking for two empty chairs. I waved. They seemed delighted to see me—or the empty chairs I had.

Amenities observed, I moved on to my questions. "I need to do some research on Agatha Christie letters. Are any missing from the house?"

They looked at each other—Ethel with her hair in a pony tail that sat on the top of her head, and Nora with her short white hair, parted on one side, with a perfect wave on the other.

Nora answered. "Stolen, you mean? I haven't heard anything about any letters missing." She looked at Ethel who shook her head and her pony tail swirled.

"Do you know who Mrs. Miller, no first name, with a London address, might be? Perhaps a cousin?"

"There are distant relatives scattered about, with an emphasis on the word 'distant,'" Nora said, "But nothing significant comes to mind."

Then Ethel spoke up. "There were five letters for sale on eBay."

"Five?" I could barely get the word out

Ethel nodded. "I considered it a low price for real ones, but if they were forged or stolen, the seller offered them cheaply, to be able to sell them quickly."

"We can ask around if you wish," Nora said, then she sighed. "Too bad Jeremy isn't with us, he could probably answer your question in detail."

The three of us mused about Jeremy and his fate, for a minute or so. I'm sure each of us had different thoughts. I only knew what mine were. But Nora was right, Jeremy would have known. We chatted a bit more, and then they went back to the docenting jobs. I pondered the eBay letters.

Nora reminded me of Miss Marple. Maybe she and Miss Marple were stereotypes—single ladies living in a village who had seen a lot in their lifetimes. And that's why Agatha Christie had used her as a main character.

Later I caught her at the end of her docent shift in the Greenway house. "I have a club meeting, but I can talk with you for a few minutes." We sat outside in the white Adirondack chairs on the lawn.

Since Jeremy's name had come up I asked her about his Christie collection as he was so knowledgeable.

"Yes, of course, very extensive as I understand, but I never saw it, nor did anyone else that I know of. He left it and the house to his niece, his sister's daughter. His niece has a son who also lives there. That would be Jeremy's grand-nephew." She told me a little more about the history of the family then she said, "I must go, my dear. I'm the Minuting Secretary and they can't start the meeting without me."

I sat there in the warm sunshine. Not hot, easy to doze off, forget the problems of the world, of why a woman was murdered.

I called Kevin's cell, or rather mobile, as it was referred to here. He was in the National Trust office on the Greenway property and could meet me at Greenway Halt for the train back to our hotel.

He told me that the police had identified the man we saw in the room. He readily admitted that he found her with a knife in her chest, and left hastily when we entered thinking we were the murderers. Kevin held back the punch line like a good storyteller. The young man's name was Lionel Chitwood. He waited for my reaction. I had none. Then he said, "He's Jeremy's great-nephew."

What! I was stunned.

After much discussion he agreed to walk me past the house that Jeremy had given his niece and great-nephew—the roof hopper. While we were talking Kevin had his back to the house so that it would look like we had just stopped to chat, not to gawk at Jeremy's building. That side of the street had apartment buildings and houses and one small hotel. The side we were on had some businesses—a hair salon, a dressmaker and a karate academy, the latter not open at the moment, but the tearoom was.

It's the English tradition when things don't go the way you want, have a pot of tea. The elegant tearoom was a replica of Charles Rennie Mackintosh's Willow Tea Room in Glasgow, circa 1903. I only know that because I read the history of it in the menu—which also listed a copious selection. I chose Assam, a strong black one, and the history of that was given also.

After giving our orders, Kevin said, "I talked with Stanley, He said he bought the letters—"

"*He* bought the letters?"

"—for his lovely wife, knowing about her Agatha Christie connection. He got them on eBay."

I told him what Ethel had said about them. "Five were offered, but by the time he bought them only three were available."

Kevin shrugged. "He bought the three, then she tracked the seller down to here. She wanted to buy the other two to complete the set. Stanley said *she* had a buyer for them. May I say that Stanley was smacking his lips at the profit."

"When and how was she able to get the buyer?"

"I asked the same question. He didn't know. Some Agatha Christie club she belonged to—a member who's a collector."

I wanted to grill Stanley, but he might ask me to London just to do a fry-up for him—whatever that was. "So she came down here to get the other two letters. If she could make a big profit with little effort, why not? Maybe Mr. Chitwood could tell us more."

"We can stop at his house and I'll leave a message."

Lionel Chitwood contacted Kevin and set up an appointment. I became Kevin's Siamese twin at the meeting, which was at the Chitwood home. We sat in an old-fashioned parlor on possibly Great Uncle Jeremy's grandmother's furniture, as it was of that period. Lionel brought in a tea tray.

He told us he had only talked once on the telephone with 'Miss Hermione,' as he called her—Madame Orange to me. They had made an appointment to meet and he had suggested the room at the Inn—where eventually they 'met,' but not as planned.

"How did you get them?" I asked.

"In Great Uncle Jeremy's collection. They were separate, tied with string, not with everything else and everything is well organized. So I thought I'd sell them. Need the pounds. Put them up for bid."

"That's what you told the police?" Kevin asked.

He nodded.

I studied the young man, guessing him to be about twenty-five, reddish hair, but that hadn't been in our description as we couldn't tell what color his hair was in the moonlight when he vaulted out of the window.

Another visit from the local constabulary, or wherever Halstead was from. He came to the Inn to question Kevin, alone, about his half-sister, but Kevin insisted I be there also, since I knew her almost as well as he did, and I had great powers of observation. Being a woman and all that. Kevin didn't say the latter. I did agree that he seemed not to notice much, but I knew he didn't voice all of his thoughts.

Halstead gave us a little news about Madame Orange. "We have found what we think is her diary, tucked away in the lining of her suitcase. Her suitcase and purse were all in a jumble, so we think the murderer was looking for something. Perhaps this." He waved a plastic evidence bag with said diary. It was small, more like a pocket calendar. And it was opened to a page. Kevin and I both leaned closer to peer at it. Halstead pulled it back.

The conversation between Kevin and Halstead brought me back to earth. That's the problem with being a writer, ever imagining the scene. Halstead let drop a couple of hints that he knew about our previous filming trips to Greenway and the trail of bodies we had left. Actually, the first trail we had nothing to do with, and he should be thankful that we helped the police uncover who the real murderer was.

Somehow all these other thoughts had given me a spurt of energy and creativity to finish the script for Kevin. I presented it to him for his review. A sterile room sure helped me get on with it. Now, in the morning, I could actually get out of my jammies, get ready and go to a hearty cooked English breakfast. Since it was buffet I didn't have to have bangers, kippers, rashers, cooked halves of tomatoes and other fine fare. Now I could swill tea until 10:30 and chow down on yogurt, muesli, fruit and my kind of good stuff. And have time to contemplate my naval—nor the oranges—but Madame Orange.

The clue, I thought, was that she was a serial liar. Taking that as a premise—that everything she said was a lie. If only I knew what her end goal was.

After Halstead's visit, I told Kevin I wanted to talk to Lionel again. I asked him to go with me, but he was committed to doing something for Peter, our director. Since they weren't actually filming for a couple of hours, I decided to visit Lionel and then go to Greenway to be on the set in case our esteemed director needed a script change. All went well as Lionel was in residence, invited me in—no tea this time, giving the hint that he didn't want me to stay long.

Lionel was getting fidgety, checking his mobile either for messages or, more likely, for the time. I had to do something fast or else I was out and wouldn't have a chance to grill him again. Time for another lie.

"When we saw you in the room holding Hermione, it seemed to me that you were checking her pockets. What were you looking for?" I never saw any such thing. "The diary? The police found it. She mentions you." Another inch grew on my nose. "You knew her long before this latest encounter. You knew too much about her to have just talked with her only once on the phone."

I was making up the scenario as I went along, but he seemed to become paler, the more I talked. "I don't think you're into making replicas, you're making originals, at least that's what you are going to sell them as. And Hermione wasn't going along with it. So you stabbed her."

"Have you told the police this?"

Whoops—I had hit the mark. "They've already guessed." I made a big jump in logic. "You know Hermione so well. She must have guessed, either when you talked on the phone as Lionel, or when you met with her, which you did. Six hours before when you stabbed her. Then came back later. I'm guessing you thought about it and decided to move the body. But you had to search her things first."

He looked around, desperate for an escape. No window to leap out of and disappear.

"Lionel…Lionel…" A weak voice came from the hallway. He jumped up. I guessed it was his mother and she sounded ill.

"You'd better go now—and take your stupid ideas with you." He rushed to the front door and opened it, waiting for me to exit. I turned and looked down the hallway. A bent over woman in a nightie with long grey hair sat slumped in a chair. His mother? I exited, the door slamming on my heel.

As I was standing there rubbing my bruised heel, a police car drove up. Halstead and Chamberlaine headed toward me—actually to the door as I was standing in front of.

"Have you come to arrest him?"

The two looked at each other. Ann Chamberlaine said, "What do you know?"

They looked at each other again. "Is he home?" Chamberlaine asked. I nodded. "Best you move on," she said—but kindly, not brusquely.

I so wanted Madame Orange to be the villain—instead she was the victim.

~The End~

GREENWAY–BACK AGAIN
A mystery short story

Kevin and I strolled the path that wound around the back of Greenway, Agatha Christie's holiday home in Devon. He wore a glued-on moustache that made him look like a thin Poirot. I wore a drab pulled-together thrift outfit from Oxfam—the drabbiest I could find and a matching drabby hat with a wide brim that sat low on my forehead. Kevin wore a hat, too, a workingman's cap, also courtesy of Oxfam.

We were in disguise.

Why?

We had been 'invited' to leave the grounds—an oxymoron if ever there was one—as we had been involved with too many bodies on the Greenway property. Not the Agatha Christie fictional ones, but real ones, murdered ones by real live murderers—all at Greenway and because of us being there. You'd think that bodies on Agatha Christie's property would be great publicity, but the powers that be thought otherwise. Hence the 'invitation.'

Kevin was our local producer, London-based, and I was a scriptwriter, Los Angeles-based. Kevin, English; me, American. We were back again, here at Greenway with an American film crew and an American, formerly English, director, Peter, who had arranged for Kevin's employment. The first film we had done in May last year was a documentary on Greenway, and its place of note in history. I had been lucky enough to be billeted here in the house, in the apartment Agatha Christie had built for her daughter and family.

Filming then had been disrupted as a murderer had been on the property. This May the team had come back again to film the story of those murders. I had written the script from my personal experience.

We were in disguise on the property to meet with two docents, Nora and Ethel, whom we knew from last year. We had questions about Agatha Christie letters, and we knew the docents knew *everything* about the author. Ethel and Nora were volunteers not National Trust employees, so we hoped they would overlook the edict given to us not to set foot on the property.

What got us started on this quest about Agatha Christie's letters was that our curiosity had been whetted yesterday when we were shown the letters the police had—Sergeant Timothy Halstead and Police Community Support Officer Ann Chamberlaine. The letters had been in the possession of a woman who claimed to be Kevin's half-sister.

In a private lounge at the Dartmouth Railway Inn, where we were staying, Ann Chamberlaine had pulled out of her briefcase four large plastic evidence bags. Two with the envelopes inside, and two with a one-page letter in each. Obviously we couldn't take them out of the plastic containers, only view both sides. I picked one with an envelope, looked at it and turned it over. On the back of the envelope was imprinted the address of Greenway. The postage imprint—put on by the post office, so no postage stamp—was smudged. They were addressed to 'Mrs. Miller' with a London address. I looked at the envelopes, front and back. They were identical in every way. "These look like they've been run through a copy machine. Both sides. No first name for Mrs. Miller?"

Chamberlaine shook her head.

I looked at the one-page letters through the plastic, and read each of them twice as though there was literal writing between the lines that only I could decipher.

Dear Cousin,

William asks to be remembered to you. Saw the school play Alan was in. Was quite good as a swashbuckling buccaneer. We all went out for dinner afterwards. Alan kept in character. Quite amusing. I will be coming up to London in a few weeks. A party for The Mousetrap. Tea at Brown's? Will ring when I get there.

With fond regards,
A

The second one read:

Dear Cousin,

Lots of rain here, the river is high. A small leak in the boathouse, but we had it repaired right away, so it is ready whenever you come down for another outing. Everything is muddy and being trailed in. Such a nuisance. We are definitely not in a desert here. Nothing like Max and my stay on digs. If only I could transport some of this rain next time we go. Hope all is still well with you. We are fine.

Fond regards as ever,
A

"The 'A' writing matches Agatha's handwriting?"

"We have experts doing a detailed analysis. We're still in the preliminary stages," she said.

"We want to know if either of you have any information about the letters," Halstead asked—their real reason for meeting with us, I was sure.

Kevin and I had shook our heads.

After they left, Kevin said to wait, as he wanted to tell me something. The 'something' was that he was quite puzzled and didn't know what it meant. "What? What?" I said, impatient with his calmness.

"It's highly unusual for the police to show evidence like that during an ongoing enquiry."

I stared at him. "That's it? It's just unusual? So what?"

"They must have permission from the Chief Constable or their superior to allow them to show them to us."

"Apparently they got permission. Come on, we have an appointment."

Now we were at the front door of Greenway. Nora stood by the open front door and I walked up to her to let her know we were here. Our disguise was complete, because she said, "Wait a moment, madam, as we have a full house. It will be about—"

"Nora, it's me," I hissed.

She looked again at me, then at Kevin, and nodded. We backtracked down the path. Our rendezvous was at The Stables, the coffee shop on the Greenway grounds. The two appeared a few minutes later riding on a Greenway golf cart, the quick means of getting around on the property.

After we exchanged greetings, I moved on to my questions. "I need to do some research on Agatha Christie letters. Are any missing from the house?"

They looked at each other—Ethel with her hair in a ponytail that sat on the top of her head, and Nora with her short white hair parted on one side with a perfect wave on the other. Ethel was a sprite, and Nora reminded me of Miss Marple. Not that she was the sleuthing type, but she had all the other characteristics.

Nora answered. "Stolen, you mean? I haven't heard anything about any letters missing." She looked at Ethel who shook her head and her ponytail.

"Do you know who Mrs. Miller is, no first name, with a London address, perhaps a cousin?"

"There are distant relatives scattered about, with an emphasis on the word 'distant,'" Nora said, "But no one significant comes to mind. We can ask around if you wish." She sighed. "Too bad Jeremy isn't with us, he could probably answer your question in detail."

The four of us mused about Jeremy and his fate, for a minute or so. I'm sure each of us had different thoughts. I only knew mine. Nora was right, Jeremy would have known, but that was definitely a dead end. "We work with what we have," I said. We chatted a bit more, and then they went back to their docenting jobs, whizzing away on the golf cart with Nora driving.

Kevin and I climbed the path again back up to the house. The path was almost a tunnel as the tree branches laced overhead. But it wasn't a dark tunnel as small sunlight pencil beams are ever moving as the breeze from the River Dart swayed them. I was hoping the spirit of Agatha Christie would be hovering around to give me inspiration.

At the house, we sat outside in the sunlight on the lawn in the white Adirondack chairs that had been a staple in Agatha Christie's day.

"You think Jeremy stole things when he worked here?" Kevin asked.

"I don't know. He was an avid collector. He could have bought the letters from someplace. It was his nephew who sold them on eBay, so if anyone stole anything it was him—but from his own uncle and he admitted as such."

"Doesn't Jeremy's sister, Mrs. Chitwood, have someone who looks after her? It was a man, I think who was the Carer." Kevin asked.

"A caregiver? You're brilliant. Yes. Do you think the caregiver might know anything?"

"Yes, that's true. I am brilliant. But don't say it too loudly. I don't want to have to sign any autographs."

I laughed. Thank goodness he had a sense of humor I could enjoy. "So far the day is a bust, we didn't find out anything from the docents."

"We did. No letters have been stolen and we agreed they know everything."

"Okay. So how do we approach the Carer?"

"I say we find out where the Carer has his elevenses and his favorite watering hole. He's bound to have one. I seem to remember a few broken blood vessels in his face, definitely the sign of a drinker."

"Aren't you the fancy detective now? Okay, lead on."

Kevin was able to find out the caregiver's—Hugh was his name—favorite watering hole named The Mooz's Head. And there was one of those hanging in the old wood-paneled pub. The story behind the name was that one of the workers on the local historical railway, and had also been in Canada also working on a railway there and had encountered a moose—only he didn't know how to spell it. The moose's head and antlers looked on the fictitious side, but I wasn't an expert on moose so I couldn't say for sure. My opinion was that it was a good replica—not looking bedraggled as one might expect a dead moose's head to look after a hundred years of hanging around.

That moose aside, the place was filled with items moose-related—salt and pepper shakers, Christmas tree ornaments—and a framed poem of *The Moose* by Elizabeth Bishop which had a place of honor, but she knew how to spell it. Of course the bar menu played up the theme—mooz meat with mooz cheese sandwiches. Fiction? Perhaps.

I stashed myself in a corner, ordered tea and chips, while Kevin plied his trade of sleuthing. I was to watch and study the subject for his body language and expressions.

Kevin was going to ask Carer Hugh about his knowledge of Agatha Christie letters. Had anyone taken any? Anything missing from the Agatha Christie memorabilia collection? Had the Agatha Christie aficionados, such as Dickie and Rickie, been around?

I sighed. The couple at the next table looked at me. Whoops, I'd better come back to earth. If Hugh said he knew nothing from nothing, then Kevin had Plan B, depending on whether he believed him or not. Also Kevin wanted to find out just what was wrong with Mrs. Chitwood. Early dementia or what?

I watched Hugh. He seemed to be enjoying himself talking to Kevin, with a pint in his hand, quite relaxed and seemed to be open, not acting or hiding something. I don't know what Kevin was saying to him, but I guessed he was asking the questions we had decided on. Hugh seemed even more expansive with a second pint. The lights in the pub were about one candlepower strong, however I could see that Hugh's face was getting flushed, not from embarrassment but from the ale.

I kept watching, nursing my pot of tea and chips, pretending to read my Kindle for the benefit of the couple next to me and anyone else who might be watching. Kevin and I hadn't come in together so I was by myself as far as anyone could tell.

Suddenly Hugh's face had a startled look. He reached to his side and pulled out his mobile. He spoke into it for a few seconds, pushed his chair back and stood. He shook hands with Kevin and strode out.

Kevin sat for a few more minutes, used his mobile that vibrated mine to signal he was leaving and we'd meet down the street.

"His relief Carer." Kevin wrangled his phone by way of explanation. "Mrs. Chitwood wanted Hugh immediately." Kevin shrugged. "Interesting guy—sergeant in the Army, then a mercenary. He's been all over the world fighting the worst kinds of blokes. He could take anybody out and leave them in pieces in a dustbin before they could say—"

"Agatha Christie."

"Ha!" Kevin said, but didn't laugh. "Hugh said he's been with Mrs. Chitwood for four and a half years. Didn't like her son, and doesn't know anything about the letters. I believe him."

"I concur."

We were standing in the street down from the pub. I was thinking what could we do next? What would Agatha Christie do? I thought of her many motives for fictional murder. A prime one was inheritance. Was financial gain involved?

At that moment Kevin's mobile rang. I only heard his part of the conversation, which wasn't much, but puzzling enough.

After he disconnected, Kevin related the other end of the conversation. A man from a branch of the Agatha Christie fan club in London wanted to talk to Kevin about some Agatha Christie letters. The man also wanted to be put in touch with Elwyn Malcroombie. He was here and could they meet? Kevin had set up an appointment.

"Must be talking about the letters my supposed sister had," he said.

The Londoners were staying at a house on the same street as Jeremy's sister, Mrs. Chitwood, which led us both to believe they had known Jeremy. It made sense because they were all Agatha Christie aficionados.

We sat in the old-fashioned dining room on possibly someone's great grandmother's quality furniture, as it was of that period, and still in good condition.

Three of them—Tweedledee and Tweedledum were the twins Dickie and Rickie, both with straining garments, vest in one case, and shirt in the other. The woman with them wore a wedding ring as did Dickie, so I made the deduction they were Mr. and Mrs. She had a pleasant face, however she apparently didn't have a name as none was given. I kept quiet in a chair against the wall, seated behind Kevin so I could watch the trio. Kevin introduced me as his assistant. I didn't have a name either, but at least I had a title.

"Let's talk about the letters. We're out several pounds and three letters and have nothing to show for it." Dickie said that in a matter-of-fact way, not angry or belligerent.

"The police have them," Rickie said.

"What about the other two letters?" Dickie's question was a monotone. "We want them, forgeries or not."

Forgeries?

"Are the letters the police have forgeries also?" Kevin asked. He sat on one side of the dining room table, the twins on the other, with Mrs. Dickie seated slightly behind them.

The twins grunted. The lady merely looked expectant as though waiting for the show to continue.

"We don't know because we've never seen them," Dickie said.

"We bought them sight unseen," Rickie added.

"Let's talk about the future letters if you're to invest in the business." Dickie continued.

The silence in the room was heavy. Finally Kevin spoke. "Gentlemen, I have no idea what you are talking about."

That was a showstopper for the other side of the table. Both men were slightly open-mouthed as they looked at each other.

"You're not going into the replica business?" Dickie asked.

"You mean replicating Agatha Christie's letters?" Kevin's voice ended in a squeak, his surprise evident.

The twins nodded.

Kevin shook his head.

The woman stood, moved to the table, opened her handbag and took out a gun. She pointed it at Kevin. I became a piece of petrified wood at one with the chair.

Now Kevin rose up slowly, stood, leaning forward with his hands on the table. "I am not in the replicating business. I do not have any letters." He was not shouting, but his words were so emphatic, spaced, that he could have been. "And I don't know an Elwyn Malcroombie."

Deadly silence again.

Then the woman put the gun back into her handbag and the scene rewound as she sat down. I was stunned that the two men had no reaction to what she had done.

"We thought you were Elwyn Malcroombie," Dickie said. Suddenly all eyes shifted to me.

"She isn't either," Kevin said. All eyes shifted back to him.

Now I really knew why he was such an effective producer. He exuded authority. He was in charge, knew exactly what he wanted. He was believable.

"All right then," Rickie said. The tension dissipated.

Kevin still stood. "Why is this Malcroombie person so important?" Kevin sat down, straight-backed, in charge as though he was conducting the meeting.

The petrifiedness in me began to ebb, drifting slowly down my body and dissipating at my toes.

Dickie reached under the table—I had visions of an even-bigger gun appearing, like an Uzi. Instead he pulled a letter out of a briefcase and slid it across the table to Kevin.

Kevin didn't touch it, just read it. I joined him and peeked over his shoulder.

Dear Sir,

I have a business proposition that should interest you greatly. I have in my possession, and have had for a number of years, several letters written by Agatha Christie herself. I would like to share my largesse with the world. Therefore I propose we go into the business of replicating them and selling them as replicas. My suggestion is that they be handwritten by someone who can duplicate Agatha Christie's handwriting. This, of course, will be set out clearly so that no hint of forgery can be attributed to us.

We are all devotees at the Agatha Christie altar and I believe we would be doing the world a service by spreading the gospel of her in making replicated letters available to all at a reasonable cost.

I leave it to you to make the necessary arrangements, and when you have done so I will make the letters available.

I will be in contact with you next week for your answer.

Most sincerely,
Elwyn Malcroombie

"Was there a return address on the envelope?"

Both Rickie and Dickie shook their heads.

"Did you research his name?"

They nodded this time.

Kevin waited. "And—what did you find out?"

"Nothing," Dickie said. "He's not listed anywhere," Rickie added.

"It says he will get in touch with you in a week for your answer." Kevin looked up. It was a question, even though I couldn't see Kevin's face.

"Tomorrow," Dickie answered.

Kevin shrugged, his hands out in a gesture of futility. "Then wait for tomorrow and all will be revealed."

"Regarding his request, and for your information, we have a good person—her handwriting is the same as Agatha Christie's. Also we need proper paper, ink and nibs. The envelopes need to be properly done so the post office stamp will show in color. We want to replicate the letters, as Mr. Malcroombie states. We won't go to prison for replicating and saying that it is so," Dickie said.

"Faithful copies of the original letters." Rickie added.

Dickie spoke. "We'll use the letters from Mr. Malcroombie, and we're hoping other collectors will participate and share their letters, so those who can't afford to buy originals will be able to buy the replicas."

There are areas of expertise I knew nothing about, such as collecting letters by famous people, how valuable they were, how one obtained them—but I didn't think the words 'share' and 'collector' were used together. I had the feeling something nefarious was going on in all of this but I couldn't identify what it was. While I was mulling over forgery and other related crimes, the others continued with their meeting.

"We can't help you, gentlemen," Kevin stated.

Mrs. Dickie's eyes slid toward me, brightening. Dickie and Rickie both looked out of lowered lids as though not wanting to acknowledge the statement. They looked at each other as though one could refute Kevin's statement.

"It's a darned good business idea, we thought. One that is completely legal," Dickie said.

"And one that will be satisfactorily remunerative," Rickie added.

"You mentioned about having a good copyist, one whose handwriting was like Agatha's—why would you need her if the letters were typed? Photocopies could be made of them," Kevin said.

"She is to hand write each letter even though they are all typed. A handwritten letter, which is word for word, like the typed one. Handwritten is more desirable and more salable." Dickie explained in a huffy manner, as though any schoolboy would know that.

"We would like to know how much you were planning to contribute, and when we can expect the money." I don't know what the expression was on Kevin's face, but it must have led Dickie to his next words. "Your sister said that you would be an investor."

"My sister!" Kevin rose from the chair again. "Let me tell you about her. She came here a few weeks ago saying she was my half sister, that my father had two families. She knew enough to make it sound plausible—" Kevin was getting emotional.

If she had been his sister, that was one thing, but if she was a con artist, that was another. I voted for con artist.

"So you see, gentlemen, she may have been making up stories. We don't know how truthful she was."

She wasn't.

The twins seemed doubtful. Mrs. Dickie's eyes were even brighter. Maybe this was the most exciting thing that had happened in her life—besides pulling out the gun.

"You are saying she's not your sister, that you aren't an investor?" Dickie asked, almost with tears in his eyes, his feelings mirrored in his brother's eyes.

"That's exactly what I'm saying," Kevin said.

"You don't have her letters?" Rickie asked. "The ones we bought from your sister?"

"As I said, the police have them," Kevin answered.

The balloon-shaped twins seemed deflated.

"The letters the police have—can you get those back for us?" Dickie asked, almost whimpering.

"No. Besides, they'll be the property of her husband. The police will give the letters back to him."

"But we bought and paid for them," Rickie said.

"Then you have to wait to talk to her husband. I can't help you. I know nothing about her dealings. And up to a few weeks ago, I knew nothing about her. Actually, I know nothing about her," Kevin told them, still sounding a little teary also.

I wondered if Mrs. Dickie was going to pull out her gun again. What possessed her to do that in the first place? Did she think Kevin was a con artist about to cheat her husband and brother-in-law? And the two men were completely calm about her actions, as though they hadn't noticed her bizarre behavior. Or were used to it. Maybe it wasn't a real gun. So far everything to do with the letters was like scenes in an asylum.

We left. The trio on the other side silent, not bidding us farewell.

"Let's get tea," I said. Across the street was a real tea place where we had been to before. Settled in, ordered, I motioned to him to continue.

"What a crazy scheme. Why do they want to handwrite everything?"

I mulled that over. "I think you've hit on something. Handwritten letters are only a step away from forgery."

"Forgery." He waved his arm and almost knocked the tray with our teapots out of the waitress' hands.

She recovered nicely and set everything perfectly on the small table. I had Darjeeling and lifted the lid on the china teapot to smell its fragrance. Loose tea. *Ah!* I stirred it gently, poured a little into the porcelain cup then sipped. Maybe sighed. "Okay, I'm ready to hear what you think they're up to."

Kevin just shook his head. We both sipped tea while it was hot.

"I wonder if your sister knew this Elwyn Malcroombe and convinced him to offer to share his collection of letters and be the one to come up with the idea."

"She would need other people like Dickie and Rickie to help with the business—help publicize, distribute, whatever it took. She couldn't do it on her own," he said.

"And she needed money. So she said you were the investor. You'd think that all of the Agatha Christie collectors would know each other—or about each other." I poured more tea into my cup.

I had a mental picture of this Elwyn Malcroombie being like Nero Wolfe, three hundred plus pounds and never leaving his brownstone, but tomorrow would be traveling to the twins' lair, possibly driven by his chauffeur or an Archie stand-in. That's the problem with being a writer, ever imagining the scene.

"Something's going on with those letters and those twin roly-poly's," I said. Suddenly I felt drained of enthusiasm for the hunt.

"You think something illegal is going to happen? Like the game's afoot?"

"The game's afoot. But I don't know what it is. To tell you the truth, I'll be glad to be leaving. I've had it with dead bodies. This has not been a merry month of May. When Peter finishes with this film—two more weeks he said—I've got my plane reservations and I'm going home. Nothing personal. I've enjoyed our time here, but I'm done. No more bodies, no more investigations—I'm outta here."

Kevin sighed, as well he should. Why was I unloading on him? He's been the best person ever to work with.

We walked back to our hotel and parted, as he was going to the drugstore, pharmacy here—promising to meet later for dinner.

Despite what I said about being *outta here*, I was still trying to figure out how a handwritten letter—not in Agatha Christie's hand—of a typewritten letter—possible in her hand, so to speak,—could be considered a replica. I wasn't in the collectible business, so maybe I just wasn't getting it. If Agatha Christie had typed the page and signed the letter 'A' at the bottom instead of a signature—it was a stretch. Then to have Agatha Christie's words set down in handwriting that duplicated her words. Not her handwriting. Too many degrees of separation.

On the other hand, what if the letter was not typed by her, or even her words? Did the twins know they might be replicating forgeries? Ironic. A writer's mind does play games, especially if you've been around Hollywood for a while.

I thought about Agatha Christie's plots. One of the reasons she was still popular, in my opinion, was that the reader could never remember who the murderer was. At least I couldn't, except for two, and I had read all of her mysteries. I remembered who the murderer was in

95

the Roger Ackroyd story—talk about the original unreliable narrator! The other murderer I remembered was the one in *The Mousetrap*. The play was touted as being the longest running play in London's theatre district. I had seen it one afternoon and was appalled at the acting, if that's what it could be called—the proverbial *they-could-have-called-it-in* performance. But I was fascinated with the story, completely taken in and didn't guess who the murderer was. The audience was always asked not to reveal the murderer's identity and probably most did as bid.

As I entered the small lobby of our hotel, Mrs. Dickie darted toward me. I didn't realize how much shorter she was than me—barely 5', and smoker-body thin. "I want to talk to you, let's go to your room."

Not wanting to be in an enclosed space with her, especially remembering about the gun, I said. "Let's talk in the lounge."

"No, no, in your room."

"My room is being cleaned that's why I'm down here."

"But you just came in," she said, eyes wide.

No fooling her. "I was out walking."

"They must be finished by now," she insisted.

She was annoying. "We don't have anything to talk about."

She grabbed my arm. "We must talk."

No, we mustn't. Just then, right on cue, Kevin walked in.

"Oh, goodie," she let go of my arm and darted to him, "You're here. Now we can start. Let's go to your room. We need to talk."

Kevin, looking unperturbed as usual, glanced at me. I shook my head and made a winding motion around my head. Didn't know if that American gesture for cuckoo translates here.

Apparently it didn't, or Kevin went with the flow as Mrs. Dickie pulled him toward the elevator. He seemed amiable to her guidance, but it's hard to read Kevin's usually placid face. He is just too good-natured. So Mrs. Dickie got her way. I wanted to peel off, go to my room, but I didn't want to leave Kevin alone with her. Something about those glittering eyes bothered me. And besides she had brandished a gun before. I decided to get my hands on her handbag and give it to her when she was exiting the Inn.

In Kevin's room—at least he had three chairs—she told us to sit. We ended up in a small triangle, our knees almost touching. She clutched her handbag in her lap. No way I could get it, unless I used brute force. "I want your sister's letters. And the money she said you'd invest." She looked at Kevin.

He leaned forward. "I don't have her letters. Or any money. I thought I made that clear."

"It was my idea." Her chest stuck out almost to bust her buttons—but she had neither. "We are going to mix real letters with the ones I will write. Your sister thought I wrote like Agatha Christie and no one would know the difference."

Delusionary.

"She told me all about you and that you were in favor of our little project. Buy the letters, which she did, and we planned to make more. We were going to be rich." She giggled. Yes, giggled—there's no other was to describe it.

Kevin's face flickered. Appalled? Shocked? Incredulous? Yes, all of those.

"Aren't your husband and brother-in-law meeting with Elwyn Malcroombie today? Doesn't he have letters you can use?" Kevin asked.

Her head went back and a cackle emanated from her mouth. She was laughing, guffawing or making some sort of hysterical reaction to Kevin's words. "Our dear Mr. Malcroombie will not be appearing. Your sister and I made him up. I wrote that letter they showed you. We had to pretend we had a source for the letters, otherwise how could we explain where we got them from? So we invented Mr. Malcroombie, a big collector who has a cache of letters." She leaned forward almost touching Kevin and whispered—actually a stage whisper—"I'm Elwyn Malcroombie."

Silence in the room except for her chuckling, but really, I want to say cackling. I'm sure Kevin was realizing with finality what a tall taleteller his supposed sister was, "I know nothing about her plans. I can't help you."

She jumped up, startling both of us. "You want them all to yourself," she screamed. "You're going to steal my idea. I'm not letting you get away with that!" She pulled the gun out of her handbag.

Damn. I should have used brute force to get her handbag away from her.

Kevin looked calm, but he couldn't have been under the situation. "Tell me about the plan."

Mrs. Dickie looked happy now, a mood shift, but she still held the gun. "Produce replicas of letters that I had written, sell them as that, but also make 'originals' and sell them as authentic Agatha Christie letters. She said she was an expert on Agatha Christie and would help me with putting in real facts in the letters. My husband and brother-in-law wanted to handle those letters, smell the ink, pretend they were living in the 1930s and really knew Agatha Christie. They wanted to sit at her table and eat with her. And I could make that happen." Her eyes were dreamy, looking into the past—or maybe the future. But she came back to the present in a snap.

"If you don't give me the letters, I'm going to shoot you."

"Shoot all you want. I don't have the letters. The police have them so I can't give them to you," Kevin said.

"Then I'll shoot your girlfriend." She pointed the gun at me.

Heart stopping. I stared at her, then the gun. It was definitely real. I had no doubt she'd pull the trigger, she seemed that desperate. And looney.

"Wait," Kevin said. "I'll give you the letters."

She turned to Kevin.

At that moment my astonishment almost took precedence over my instinct for survival. But not quite. I lunged for her gun hand. My stunt work training came in handy. She was stronger than I expected. I grabbed her gun hand, twisting it but being sure the barrel pointed away from us. She tried to claw me, but Kevin grabbed her other arm. I was able to get the gun away from her. We tied her hands behind her back, taking kicks to the shin. She was a tiger.

"Call Halstead." I yelled at Kevin even though he was about a foot away. I watched her and rubbed my bruised shins. Next he called hotel security and two ex-wrestlers appeared. They had a place to put her until the police came. In spite of her accusations of kidnapping, torture, and a variety of other things that we had supposedly done to her within the last ten or fifteen minutes—interspersed with blue words—they carted her off without a question. Maybe our reputations had preceded us, or they knew about her antics. Either way I was glad to see her derriere disappear with the two men. She did not go gently.

I sank back into the chair. Kevin had disappeared then reappeared with two sodas that had enough sugar in it to help combat the adrenaline surge and ebb that had left me shaky.

Halstead and Chamberlaine arrived and had Mrs. Dickie escorted out—maybe to Reading Gaol, but that was too much to hope for.

Dickie and Rickie apparently were innocents. They only knew about the replicas. They were led to believe that the originals would be loaned by Elwyn Malcroombie. And, yes, they did have sources of ink, paper, from whatever decade they decided the letter was written. A very neat operation.

I bid a fond farewell to Kevin. I would miss him, but I was more than ready to leave Greenway, and was happy to board the plane with Peter and the rest of the film crew.

Alas, on the plane, Peter asked me about the letters. Was there a story in it? Could I write the screenplay and we would all go back next year and film at Greenway. Ha! I told him there was no story, just some rumors that turned out to be just that. A tempest in a teacup. I pulled the eyeshade over my eyes and went to sleep.

~The End~

Printed in Great Britain
by Amazon